OVERLAP

THE LIVES OF A FORMER TIME JUMPER

N JOSEPH GLASS

ISBN: 979-8860388437

1 | The Seed

THE puddle expanded like oil—dense, stretching outward with a darkness as metaphorical as it was black. Its volume challenged the hope within my desperation, but I fought to hold on to it as if it could affect reality—by sheer force of will. Gloving my hand as it raised from her side, the thick liquid dripped crimson with flashes as embers of a dwindling fire glinting in the misty rainfall under the dim streetlight.

I saw two men, as my cloudy head could recall. They came so abruptly out of nowhere. The details blurred like an old memory while it happened in slowed time. At that moment, I had no idea what they could have wanted. We never presented our financial or social status in public. My dearest love didn't relish attention and kept any flash or pomp far removed from her. We were nobodies, blissfully strolling home in the rain after a simple dinner in a modest restaurant in a safe but not overly posh part of town. At least we thought it was safe before this night.

I offered them my money, watch, whatever they wanted, they could freely take, without resistance. Initially, I admit, I considered the mental image flashing a scene of me heroically saving my wife as a damsel in distress, even though I had no training in hand-to-hand fighting or self-defense. Quickly, I squashed the notion, having learned that in most cases, a compliant surrender would mean the loss of a few meaningless items, some money, but allow you to go on with your life. To stay alive. And that was my solitary goal. No one ever told me the odds of both of us doing that.

The lead man clutched a handgun—I still see its substantial, thick barrel—as he eyed the watch with a disappointed grimace. Nervously waving a small pistol, the other removed my trembling partner's necklace and yanked the ring from her finger—made of 14-carat gold but scarcely worth a few hundred dollars. Horrified eyes watched the anguish drip from her face for the loss valued in sentimentality her willful submission brought. She had always cherished her wedding band—cheap, gold-plated, and all I could afford when we wed. The necklace held higher monetary worth, the first-anniversary gift that set me back two hundred fifty dollars after saving for months. We were university students and barely scraping by back then.

My hand reddened her chestnut curls as it brushed them back over her ear to reveal her always glowing, symmetrically beautiful face. The other side pressed into the concrete.

"Ellie," I said gently. "They're gone. You're going to be okay. I've dialed 911. They're coming. You'll be okay. It's over."

From her blank gaze, I surmised she hadn't realized she'd been shot, the shock and pain not written on her face. Nothing there. I had learned to read her so well in our twelve years together but saw no expression, thoughts, or feelings advertised only for me to see in the deep wells of her hazel eyes.

Blank.

"They're coming. You'll be fine. It's over," I muttered through my tears, my eyes blinking from the droplets of rain breaking through my lashes. "You'll be okay. It's over."

A simple mugging ended in the shaky man's nervous finger retracting. Vividly clear in my mind, I can never forget the look of shock overlaying his countenance as if he couldn't understand why the cold metal in his hand had jerked it. The men vanished, having fled into the darkness of the mist to disappear from the streetlight's ghostly glow. The ambulance had arrived, and the paramedics were immediately in action, urgent in their movement. It was over. I was correct about that.

On that night, in my rain-soaked dinner suit under the haunting yellow glow of a streetlight-turned-memorial marker, my dear Ellie expired.

Before I rose to my feet under the pull of the paramedic's arms, I had already devised my plan.

2 | The Recluse

"NO, young lady. I never remarried."

The woman in my private study looked to be at that age when people of my years said things like, 'She's old enough to be your daughter.' Given the decades of a man's procreative abilities, that simplistic description fit thousands of people I would pass on the street each day—though I seldom ever left the house in recent years. Beyond the biological fact of my sperm being able to fertilize the egg inside her mother to produce the lovely Jessica Mathews over thirty years ago, I had already been widowed by then and had vowed to only myself to remain celibate. So, you see, I couldn't have been a father to any of those thousands I only theoretically passed on the street.

A sympathetic gaze covered the eager reporter's eyes. "May I ask why?"

"Well…" A slit in my chair's worn crimson leather sighed as the topic fidgeted me some. "They say it's better to have loved and lost than never to have loved at all. I supposed there's truth in that. But to make that *my* truth, I must add how such a love could never be replaced. To honestly say Ellie was the love of my life… she remains the only one."

"And is her death what started you on your work? Did you devote two decades of your life to inventing time travel in hopes of saving her?"

Though I paused in contemplation, I'd had the answer ready for forty years. "Could there have been a nobler motivation?"

"I admit, I didn't expect such romantic notions when this interview began. I had learned, of course, of your wife's tragic death and assumed it was part of the impetus. But as your work has made you one of the world's wealthiest people, I assumed financial gain drove you to hide in a lab for nineteen years."

It left me strangely intrigued how Miss Mathews set the tablet on the sofa cushion beside her and jotted the odd point here or there in a paper notebook with a pencil. Indeed, she must have wondered why I granted her, of all people, this interview.

"Hide myself?" She was clever, carefully considering her words but shooting them out in feigned spontaneity. I'd chosen well. "And what do you suppose I missed out there in the real world? I endured the Trump and Biden years but happily avoided the mess that came not long after. Turns out the world is still steeped in prehistoric human mentality."

I crossed my legs and raised my glass to float smokey notes of my favorite Islay whisky through stimulated nose hairs, studying the squint my words pressed onto the reporter's eyes.

"To this day, we have yet to find a cure for the cancer of racism in human society. I missed the riots over unification with the U.K. and the obliteration of three Islamic states. No, Miss Matthews, financial gain had nothing to do with me *hiding* myself, as you said."

"You really see the world through such a cynical lens?"

"Oh, it's a well-earned negativity, as any thinking person would agree. I merely mean to convey to you my true motivations. You see, my inventions were not driven by profit, and my only splurging of any prosperity from there has been this home."

Jessica Matthews uncrossed her legs and set her forearms on her thighs. "This house, lovely as it is, doesn't seem much of a splurge, Mister Hollister."

"Miss Matthews, Jessica, let's dismiss the formalities. Call me Marcus. I may have the years and grays to go with them but believe me, I do *not* merit such respect."

"But sir…" She straightened in her seat. "Your accomplishments changed the world. Created a new industry, an entirely new and safe means of recreation and vacationing, improved our nation's military, and made you filthy rich. And you live in isolation in this modest four-room home in the middle of nowhere."

"What is the point of money and fame but to buy the life one wishes to live? I'm not a total hermit. Reclusive, yes, but if you thought you'd be the first human I've seen in years, I'm sorry to disappoint. I have a cook three evenings and a housekeeper one day each week."

"Friends? Family? You were more open in your dealings after your years in the lab. You ran a multi-trillion-dollar corporation and contracted for the military. The world knew you for a time—before your reclusive ways returned."

"Family?" I must have drifted in contemplation considering the word. Jessica waited. One of the points I liked about her style—and I had rewatched her interviews, studying her—is her giving the subject time to collect thoughts and answer her questions or respond without feeling obligated to fill the awkward gaps of silence carved into the conversation.

Conversation. Yes, I wanted to have a dialogue, not to be interviewed. And Jessica Matthews had shown herself to be a master conversationalist more than a deep-cutting interrogational journalist.

"Ellie. She was all the family I had. I know you've done your homework before coming to see me. My childhood in foster homes has been well-documented."

"Friends? Your former partner? Coworkers? Do you have any social interactions beyond your home staff?"

The scotch whirlpooled in the tumbler as my closed eyes aimed themselves at the ceiling. Jessica hadn't even asked about the internal twilight cast from the one dim lamp when she arrived and took her seat. Curious eyes scanned my bookcase as she took a quick inventory of the four hundred books lining two opposite walls.

Did she hope to learn something about me by the written word in my possession? Perhaps. I had to concede the approach sound. A complete profile of a man could be constructed by such means. Of course, that man would not be me as I hadn't read half of those textbooks and none of the novels.

"There, you listed three very diverse categories." I smiled warmly at the lovely young lady. "My former partner was never a friend, not even when things were good between us. Coworkers were subordinate suck-ups. Sycophantic leeches latched onto whomever had the richest blood."

Memories of those years pinched the back of my throat more than the inhaled mouthful of Lagavulin tingling my taste buds.

"Friends?" Jessica matched my forward lean as if a prized secret were about to be slipped into her ears only. We were alone. "I've never been particularly good at making those. You've heard that adage: you need to be a friend to have a friend. Well, I guess I was never much good at being one."

"Marcus. How long has it been?"

"You mustn't speak in riddles, dear girl. You may be direct with me. I prefer it."

"When was the last time you left this house?"

"Oh, I think you've taken an incorrect perception of me. I leave the house every day, rain or shine."

The reporter pulled her heart-shaped face back and brushed a lock of brown hair behind her ear. My mind flooded with images, the yearning inside me that called her to my home. A raging torrent of memories swept me away from the moment. The resemblance had caught me off guard, eerily more than expected.

"That's not how I've heard it. And no one has seen you for over twenty-two years. Outside of your staff of two, that is. So where do you go each day?"

"You marveled at the modesty of this home. It is exactly what I need if even a bit more. I have a room to sleep, this study, the kitchen and dining areas, and, of course, the bathrooms. But it took you forty-five minutes to reach my home in my private pod tube, which is why this house is my home."

"Privacy. You live in the middle of this preserve to be left alone?"

"What else could a man with no family or friends desire? I walk the grounds daily, and my sole recreation, my escape, is in my garden. My entire diet comes from my toiling. I tamed that soil and have lived off the land for years."

Jessica jerked her head higher off her shoulders as a gong-like blast roiled in. As if on cue—I did signal it just then for dramatic effect—my chef crashed some pots on the kitchen counter.

"My chef. Please, you will share a meal with me and sample the fruit of my labors."

"*Oh*. That's most kind, but I've only scheduled an hour for this interview. I don't wish to impose."

"It is already done. The vegetables and grains are grown, and the chef is preparing. You see, that I typically do not *have* company does not, by default, mean I never *wish* it."

3 | The Motivations

AFTER a vicious head wag, the coughing started. Perhaps I shouldn't have pushed Jessica to join me the third time, but having my second drink with her having none seemed socially unacceptable.

"I think a lighter aperitive would have been more suitable to your taste."

"It tastes like pure smoke. Who could drink that?"

"Thank you, Guillaume." My astute chef came quickly with water in response to Jessica's violent efforts to hack up the lingering effects of the scotch. "How much longer?"

"Dinner will be served at seven, as requested."

Carefully trickled information gave the reporter what she hadn't come to learn, teasing some details to heighten curiosity and stimulate the proper response to my later proposal. Of course, I knew she cared little about my work's technical process and challenges. So many had told those tales over the years. Peter leaked those details like a sieve when every news agency from everywhere beat down our door for interviews. Type my name or 'Peter Andrews' into any search engine, and thousands of detailed articles will fill your head with that dribble.

I needed a hook, some bait to keep her interest peaked.

"Of course, Peter and I had vastly different motivations."

"He was all about the money, wasn't he?"

"*Yes,* would be the correct answer, but, simultaneously, terribly inadequate. Yes, he was in it for the money, but he loved the fame even more."

"How did you come to be partners then?"

My mouth stretched into a wide smile. "I knew you came for what hasn't already been written, video recorded, blogged, or spewed over social media."

"Sir, Marcus, I'm here to learn *who you are.* Everyone knows what you've created and the basics of how. At least at a high enough level to keep it proprietary. And the world knows enough about Peter Andrews."

"True, true. But the world starts with the machine and the business it spawned. Peter and I started much before that. We met at university and tossed business ideas around until one stuck with both of us. Nothing 'sexy,' as Peter would say. Our first project, subsidized by the depths of Peter's trust fund, made a simple AI-based network routing system that transformed existing data connections to instantaneous synchronous flow channels, making possible the growth of the metaverse and its successor, *Transcend*."

While the world knew *trænSɛnd*—its pretentious spelling to swell its swagger—with ninety percent of the population plunged into the immersive virtual world daily, few cared how *Tomorrow's Now Incorporated*, Peter's company, provided the backbone to make it work. Built on my quantum intelligence subsystem, of course.

"And that's how you funded *Vacations in Time?*"

"Oh, you're skipping quite a few years there, Jessica. While the proceeds from that first project could have set me and Peter for life, he wanted to throw it all into funding the next big thing."

"Which was?"

"You've done your homework. But research, no matter how thorough, is only as good as the source material. Right? You knew what I told you and how it—eventually—funded

Vacations in Time. What you wish to know is what no one else knows."

With deep satisfaction, I watched the sparkle in Jessica's eyes brighten. I started into the territory she yearned to explore, to report something no one had, to get the exclusive. Simply speaking with me gave her that. It was the only interview I had ever granted in all my years.

"There was a gap of several years, reportedly filled exclusively with the time such a breakthrough took to develop and test. But you say there was something else between *Tomorrow's Now* and *Vacations in Time*?"

"Several something else's. All failures. Until the biggest failure led to our greatest success."

I had her. A deep hunger dilating her pupils gave her away.

A reverberating metal twang entered the room, signaling the meal had been set on the table right on time at 7 p.m. The timing could not have been better. Jessica's appetite for the story rivaled my stomach's pleading for the Slow Cooked Duck with Perigord Black Truffles as its decadent aroma wafted into the study.

I escorted my lovely young guest to the dining room, where we sat across the oval table without words as Guillaume lifted each sterling silver cloche dome off our plates and explained the meal.

"I thought you lived off the land. I expected a vegan meal."

"Ducks live on the land." My hearty laughter induced the same from Jessica.

We spoke of light subjects while eating, me insisting on no 'shop talk' at the table. I told her my favorite foods and wines, and she reciprocated hers.

In a casual tone, Jessica tried for more. "When was the last time you left the preserve?"

"What did we agree about dinner conversation?" Open to the topic, I had to goad her a little and not make it too easy. Ellie always hated it when I did that.

"This isn't work. As we're getting to know each other now, I'm curious."

Fair enough. I'd gotten her to tell me more about herself over the table than I revealed about my life. Stories of her early years in journalism intrigued me. How she worked so hard, put in all the grunt work for years—correcting her slip of tongue fumbling out the word weeks—and how she funded her internet channel when no one would give her an anchor position. Not even ranked in the global media ratings, she sounded almost ashamed to be interviewing me—an exclusive the most famous seasoned reporters would kill or die to get.

"Fair enough. Eleven years, *almost*." Wheels spun, and I saw it over her face like a 'Please wait, I'm thinking' sign.

"You attended Peter's funeral?"

A smirk and head nod gave her my reply.

"No one reported that. How did nobody see you? Wait, did you attend in Transcend?"

"You asked when I left the property. I was there, in the flesh. No one had seen me in years, and then few photos of a much younger me ever circulated. It didn't take much to disguise myself."

"But you hated each other by the time he kil—I mean… when he died."

"No need for subtleties. Everyone knows he took his own life in the end. He died a miserable, lonely man swinging from a rope in his Monaco penthouse. You see, money and fame seldom equal happiness."

"What about you? You're as much alone, or more."

"And mostly miserable. But my misery comes from a single loss. Don't worry; I won't tie it to a rope to extinguish it. It is mine to carry until I die—of natural causes—like liver failure."

My laughter placed too high a demand on my lungs and turned into a wheezing cough.

"I never hated Peter. Media types like… sorry. It was exaggerated in the media. Besides, I went to offer condolences to his sons. Say what you will about that money-loving, two- and three-timing scoundrel; his kids shouldn't inherit their father's sins."

"Sins. I need to explore that a good bit deeper."

4 | The Failures

"IF YOU mean to continue the interview, we should return to the study. I only take interviews in my Chesterfield."

"Chesterfield?"

"My chair. No one smokes anymore, so calling it a smoking chair seemed pointless. Calling it my drinking chair or the Lagavulin chair sounds eccentric and too limited for everything the chair is good for."

An extended elbow invited the enthusiastic young lady's arm, and we sashayed into the study to let her return to the business part of her visit. It had been some time since I'd had such pleasant company.

One crystal glass turned a glorious burnt amber with two generous fingers as I thought it best not to offer Jessica a repeat. Besides, Lagavulin 32 wasn't to be wasted.

Settling into her seat, Jessica yawned and stretched. Too early for the offer. Let her dig, keep fueling her lust for more.

"So, you have a good relationship with Peter's boys? You keep in touch?"

"No. I barely knew them while Peter and I worked together. They wouldn't recognize me if they saw me."

"Did they? See you at the funeral? You said you went for them."

"One of a thousand random people in a line of condolers."

"You went out, once in two decades, for *that*?"

"It was the right thing to do."

"Okay. Let's get back on point, shall we? You and Peter had failures, you said. Tell me about those."

"I had failures in the lab. That caused Peter to fail with the venture capitalists. We tried to create a teleportation chamber and then an anti-gravitation device. Those were expensive failures, and Peter started losing patience. Ellie kept me positive. She was always encouraging about my work, though she didn't understand it. A brilliant mind for law but had no desire to lend any of it to such technical trifles."

When my hand raised the tumbler, I had no thirst to quench. Thoughts of my dear love tasted less bitter going down with a hefty swallow of my favorite single malt.

"And that's when I lost Ellie. I lost myself. I lost everything. Peter tried to be understanding, but after a week, he pushed and pushed for me to get back to work. He'd sunk a fortune into the anti-grav R and D and desperately fought to hold the investors at bay."

"That's when the issues between you two began?"

"They were always there. But this didn't help. I took a month off and traveled through Europe. With a cleared head, I got to work, but the project was a bust. There was no way to make the thing work as we had stretched quantum theory and fringe physics to the limit and couldn't lift more than a paperclip."

"That's when you moved on to *Vacations in Time*?"

"*Vacations in Time*. You keep saying the words like it was some great accomplishment. No, that was Peter. He did what he did best: turning a failure into a profitable business."

"Failure? It was your greatest invention. It's why you're a household name and one of the most successful people on the planet. How was it a failure?"

"I'll not debate the many meanings of the word 'successful.' My mind wasn't in the game after Ellie. I don't think the anti-grav would ever have worked, even with me at full capacity. I had determined that night, while leaning over my dear Ellie's body, to use everything I knew or could learn about quantum physics and fringe science to do what so many others had failed before me to accomplish. I would invent time travel."

Jessica leaned forward and took my hand. "To save your wife."

My hand sprung back from under hers; too much. No, I had no immoral intentions, no desire beyond satisfying a morbid curiosity. Still, the hand, that almost forgotten yet familiar contact …

"Yes. I would go back in time and save Ellie. Never walk down that street. Only, time travel didn't exist. So, I had to create it."

"As we all understand, this was never possible. And this had always been presented to the public as such. Your invention was unveiled as a recreational tool, nothing more."

"Peter. He saw the potential in our failure. Marketing it that way, he created *Vacations in Time*. No, it wasn't possible. And, as a result, here I sit in this house. Alone. I tried and kept trying. I stuck with it for years, doing nothing else, barely sleeping. It worked. Only—it didn't."

"Why? What did you find in your research and tests?"

"I had it." I had the reporter. "We built a small prototype, about the size of my minifridge here, and I took an object and sent it back in time. At least, we thought so. See, to send something back and know it worked, we had to have seen the object already before we sent it, right?"

"Okay. I'm following." I could see she was. Jessica had brains to go with the charm and radiant, perfectly proportioned face. "How did you prove it? Did the object disappear?"

"That's just it, they never did. I tried sending small objects and recording video of the time we'd sent them back to, assuming we'd see two of them for a few seconds if it worked."

Wide eyes glued to me, no notes written on the reporter's notepad.

"We saw nothing at first. So, we slowed the playback during the few seconds of assumed time overlap."

"Overlap?"

"Yes. We never saw two objects, but I was certain it was working. I believed we were sending things back and explained to Peter the objects must have overlapped. The one that traveled back in time overlaid the one traveling forward through normal-time."

"How? How did you figure that?"

A sip of scotch made its way from my glass to generously wet my mouth. I had never spoken of this to anyone. The exhilaration filled me like a drug in an explosion of endorphins, taking thirty years off my tired bones.

"You've heard of folding time and space. The space part doesn't work, but folding time does. And as with a sheet of paper, the folded part can only reach as far as its opposite edge, its beginning. Stretch it farther, and the pieces no longer touch or overlap. I discovered I could send something back, but only in its own timeline, where it entered an overlap."

"As if two versions merged into one at a single point in time in the past?"

"In *its* past, yes." This Jessica Matthews had a brilliant mind to follow that so well. "We continued through the night. We had no idea what would happen if we sent something to a time before considering using it. It took me three days of tests to realize my machine worked over greater times, regardless of location. The objects could travel to themselves wherever they were at that time—but only in their past."

"You invented time travel. You could send something to the past."

"Yes. Sort of. The next test was to alter the future of an object from within a jump to its past."

5 | The Overlap

JESSICA held her own, trying to follow complex theories unfolding into the realities I expounded. In truth, it sounded like fantasy or the ravings of a lunatic. If not for the notoriety of *Vacations in Time*, no one would have indulged me as she.

Piping hot tea couldn't be sipped just yet, but I noticed a comfort in the reporter's relaxed cheekbones as she held the cup. My staff told me I kept it too cold in the house. To me, the rain pelting the vast picture window that filled most of the outer wall had christened Jessica's evening chill.

"At this point, you successfully sent tiny objects back into themselves, in the same place as they were, and they came back *unchanged*. Your goal was to alter the past. Did you consider it a failure at this point?"

"Quite the opposite. I had designed and built a device that could send objects through time. Now, to measure the level of success, we needed to make an impactful change to our present by something we sent back to the past."

"How did you accomplish that?"

"I created a small… bomb, I guess, with a tiny bit of explosive powder that would do nothing more than leave a burn mark on a wooden table. We set it on the table for an hour, then I set a timer to detonate and sent it back." Anxious eyes held in suspense on the reporter's face awaited the result. "Nothing. The device came out of the machine having detonated, but the table where it overlapped had no burn marks."

"How could you know if it detonated in the chamber or on the table in the past?"

"Excellent question. Even Peter asked the same. There was only my stubborn insistence that my invention must have worked; my calculations were flawless. To prove it, to know what happened in an overlap, we needed to see how a living creature would react."

"Marcus, you know that animal trials had been outlawed long before you began, even those decades ago. And I've never read or seen any reports on you doing this."

My read on Jessica lost its certainty, though it became readily evident she didn't care for the animal experimentation we had done. Ellie wouldn't have allowed it. At the time, we considered it a necessary part of the process and let the care taken for the creatures soothe our consciences.

"You're an intelligent person, Jessica. And you've seen much in your field of work. People didn't ask the questions they didn't want answered. They wanted to jack into our fantasy world for a guilt-free adventure in time—in a memory, old or new. Let me skip to the chimps. Oh, we built a larger machine, about the size of a shower box."

Smokey notes reminded me how I nursed the glass fidgeting in my hand, its contents satiating only my nostrils.

"We needed to know what a mind experienced during the overlap. How it would come out on the other side."

"I assume you found a way to know what's on a chimpanzee's mind?"

"In a way, yes. We exposed our chimp, Georgie, to calming music and noted the brainwave patterns." Jessica giggled at the chimp's unusual name. "We did this for days and logged consistent results."

"Then you exposed him to the calming music before going into the machine during the overlap?"

"Not right before. We needed to be certain Georgie experienced something while in the past that he hadn't in normal-time. So, we taught him how to push a button for the soothing music. He loved it and pushed it over and over. The trick was *not* having him activate it in normal-time." I swirled the cold glass, dragging my thumb up and down the ridges of the sculpted crystal, then took a swig. "So, we put him in a room and let him push that button to his heart's content, waited for the brainwaves to settle, then put him in the machine set to go back to when he was in that room."

My playful pause aimed to heighten anticipation and intensify the moment. Memories of Ellie kicking me under the table for doing that to her friends pained my shin.

"*And?*"

It worked. Jessica's desperation for the story to continue invigorated me like adrenaline.

"His brainwaves showed the same patterns as when he heard the music. He came out with the memories of his overlap intact."

"Then you successfully created impactful time travel. The results proved that you altered his past."

"No, that's just it. It hadn't changed when I checked the computer logs for the number of plays. The music player had played the song four times before Georgie entered the machine. After his overlap, in which we knew he played it again, the log again showed only four plays."

"What did all that prove?"

"No cat in the box. Confirmation of my earlier conclusions: we couldn't change the past. For decades, physicists argued the nature of time and the possibilities of traveling through it—more to the point, alteration of time. You've heard that babble—ripping a hole in the fabric of the time-space continuum, the butterfly effect, step on the wrong twig?" I watched for her careful half-nod. "Nonsense. Nothing changed, except for the memories of the traveler's time in the overlap."

"This is where some early skepticism had been raised against your machine and the claims of the service it provided. Some called it nothing more than a cleverer form of *Transcend*—virtual reality built on memories and not time travel."

"You did indeed do your homework, young lady. Peter spent a fortune keeping that out of the news."

"I'm sure. So, this led to something you didn't expect or plan—a completely new version of altered reality. In *Transcend*, I can create a virtual or augmented environment, and the AI can take all the input I can provide to build a memory. Plenty of people do it—I've done it. People can relive that memory with decently vivid realism. What made *Vacations in Time* different?"

"The reality."

Yes, okay. I intentionally placed that on the cliff, leaving her in suspense. The temptation to enjoy this experience couldn't be sidestepped. That drove Ellie crazy when we first met, and she promptly forbade me to do it to her since our first date. I snuck some in here or there. While she protested each time, I saw the corner of her mouth lift as she tried to hide the smile. I observed it now in Jessica Matthews' contemplative sneer as much as in the memory.

"You see, Jessica, there was no 'virtual' in the reality we created for people. We sent clients back in time. The scents, sights, sounds, and feelings were as real as in normal-time. As real as this moment. If I sent you back a few hours, you'd taste that meal again, savor the flavors, and delight in the aromas. You would not be experiencing a memory but *reliving* that moment."

"And I could… change how I did it the first time? Say I wanted less duck to have a bigger piece of that amazing torte—I could do that in the overlap?"

"That's the whole point. If someone wanted to relive a perfect moment, they could do it in exactly the same way, again and again. But, they could also try to do it better by attempting something different to see how it would have turned out."

"And when they exited the chamber, your machine, nothing in the present would have changed."

"You've just summed up my greatest failure."

"You couldn't save her. There was no way to change what happened to Ellie."

"Exactly!"

6 | The Night

DARKER than night, the storm's ferocity had entered the study, rattling Jessica's bones. I placed a sofa blanket around her shoulders and refilled her herbal infusion. I called it tea, and she politely corrected me. I'd had enough scotch and needed to keep a clear head, not forget myself, or my advanced years, to the moment.

An hour, she had said. It had now been about six. *A forty-five-minute pod ride to the road where her car awaited, then more than an hour to her hotel from there, even on the express airway at this hour.* I didn't wish the experience to end. It was time for the offer I'd primed her to accept.

"I'm afraid it has gotten quite late, and the storm shows no signs of settling soon. Please, be my guest for the night, so I needn't worry about your safe arrival home."

"*Oh.* Well, I think I should go… you don't even have a guestroom."

"You are in the guestroom. You see bookshelves lining two walls, this marvelous panoramic window here, and one suspiciously blank wall."

"I did notice that."

"That opens to an ensuite guestroom. Never used, but always equipped with clean bedding and toiletries."

"I don't know."

Apprehension filled her. I could see it overtaking her countenance. She didn't know me, and people often equated a recluse with a madman who would kidnap her and keep her prisoner. *Could she think that of me?* Too many films and stories may have shaped her fears for this night.

"The room locks from inside, and I'm a sound sleeper. I'd very much like to continue this conversation. We have so much more to discuss, and I have so much more to share that I know you'd like to hear. Please, be my guest."

"I didn't bring anything. I…"

"Not to worry. As I said, the ensuite is fully equipped. There's a night dress, an assortment of clean clothes, fresh bedding, and anything you need in the bathroom."

She looked out the window at the distant lightning through trails of rain snaking down the glass, bombarded by thick drops from the torrential downpour.

"O… okay. Most kind. I think it would be difficult to travel home in this. And I *would* like to hear more. We haven't gotten to the business, the clients, and why you shut it down. And since all your machines have been dismantled, I guess I won't be able to relive this moment to get anything I miss the first go-around."

Jessica smiled. I could see she had settled, now more at ease about staying the night.

With the press of a button, the bare wall split down the middle and slid apart. Widened eyes marveled at the spectacle of the hidden room as the reporter gawked at the bed and furnishings. Five-star hotels didn't offer the luxury of my guest suite. Given the simple décor of my home, it must have come as a surprise.

While I cared not for such frivolous indulgences, I considered how she would. Ellie never aspired to such, but it didn't mean she couldn't enjoy it occasionally. Jessica didn't need to know I had renovated my panic room just for her, for this one night.

"Help yourself to anything in the kitchen. There's bottled water in the bar beside my desk if you like. The phone beside the bed is a direct connection to me. Just lift it if you need anything else, any time."

After I showed her how to lock the door, assuring her the physical mechanism could only be opened from the inside, I bade her goodnight.

Ellie hated lying and didn't tolerate being lied to—ever. She always caught me, too, so I gave up trying early on to save our relationship. Something about how a good partner completes a person tickled the synapses with each memory, rationalizing my life's emptiness without her.

I never slept soundly, not much at all. This night would be worse than all others. I had no immoral intent, as mentioned. I'm an aged man; the drive for such things perished some time ago. Curiosity, a burning deep inside for a connection impossible to ignore, invited shame to stay the night.

On the edge of my bed, I waved my hand to activate the projectors. While observing her new and unexpected surroundings, Jessica Matthews filled the room around me. Few people have this version of *trænSɛnd* or even know of its existence. Privacy laws and strict augmented reality regulations forbid it. The system's total immersion had put me in the room, unraveling the reality around me while falling short of the solidity of an overlap—the smells. While *trænSend*'s emitters tried to mimic them, the fabricated scents always gave it away. Even this advanced—and illegal—version offered only a limited sensation beyond the visual.

Gracefully, she floated around me... an angel's form with a symmetrical face. I saw only my beloved when Jessica pushed a curl behind her ear to gaze unobstructed over the assortment of garments in the wardrobe. She pulled on one of Ellie's nightgowns—blue satin with black lace. While the modesty filter would allow my guest into it with dignity, I closed the connection.

Youthful eyes watched a majestic cherub glide across the floor from the wardrobe to the shower. No, not Jessica, and not with these dulled, lifeless eyeballs. I'd left the projectors off and saw only my Ellie in a mental image assembled more from conjecture than remembrance. Under my eyelids, my lost love stared at me, a goddess ready for bed but not sleep. Longing for a memory kept my eyes tightly sealed.

Mental processes running on their own shifted to wondering what was racing through Jessica's mind—the lust that terrified my imagination of this night hadn't arrived; the years had taken it from me.

I showered and dressed for bed.

Lying on my back, I imagined Jessica's every toss and turn just as I used to watch my Ellie drift into slumber. She always fell asleep before me. Did my enigmatic guest have a similar light snort when she turned onto her back? My vanished love's bed noises gently reverberated in my ears. Never an irritant, not like my snoring was to her.

Startled to consciousness by booming thunder, I worried for Jessica. When I switched on the projector to check on her, she wasn't there. A rush of panic filled me with morbid dread. What could have happened? Groggy, my senses returned to me and told me she must have been in the restroom. No. An open door, no light. Where had she gone?

Hurriedly, I sat up to see a silhouette in the picture window. Jessica stood still as a statue, somber as a ghost, mesmerized by the continual rainfall that had eased into a gentle drizzle. Standing beside her, I joined in the wonder. Occasional lightning turned the sky white and illuminated Jessica like a spotlight. She was the star performer on the stage. She darkened again for the moment it took for the night view to adjust.

This felt wrong. Jessica was in her nightgown and as lovely as Ellie. Me beside her, unknown to her. An invasion of her privacy, her dignity. It *was* wrong. I stood beside her, studying her, the lines of her face carving out her cheeks, the jawline coming together to cradle her gently dimpled chin.

Ellie never cared for her chin or her nose. Regardless of my best efforts, she may not have known how elegantly exquisite I found her to be despite them. Jessica's face had no such imperfections.

Jessica Mathews—the curiosity in my home.

Uncanny. That's the word I used when I first saw her three weeks ago reporting from London. I must have watched the interview with that CEO a hundred times. (I tuned in only because it was one of Peter's sons.) I returned to verify what the photos and holograms had already confirmed against my vivid memories.

Finally, she was here. We met. Honestly, I had no idea what I expected beyond the interview and spending the following day together to extend our time as long as possible. Something so right, so true and natural stirred within me. A part of me awakened, taking some of the emptiness away.

My story should be told, and it needed to be told by Jessica Matthews.

I returned to bed and drifted into memories that became dreams.

7 | The Next Day

JESSICA woke. I had been awake for close to an hour and watched her sleep. The joy of seeing her in physical reality and continuing our conversation fought for dominance over the loss of the moment—my memories having placed me beside Ellie in peaceful sobriety. I had to pull myself from our bed, leaving my Ellie there as her day began later than mine. That had never been an easy feat.

The reporter-turned-houseguest found me at the dining table, fresh fruit and yogurt laid out and coffee in the decanter. A hand settled gently over my shoulder, and a warm smile glanced over me. Jessica couldn't have known just how Ellie greeted me in the morning. Had she established why I chose her for the only interview I'd ever allowed? Jessica had done her research. She said nothing.

The dress she had chosen, my Ellie's dress, flowed over her body like a springtime afternoon.

"Good morning, Jessica. Slept well?"

"Very. Thank you. That bed is a cloud of heaven. Thunder woke me at one point, and I stared at the rain over the field, the lightning turning the sky into fire. It was spectacular."

"I did as well, for a few minutes. Did not having curtains disturb you?"

"At first, yeah. In the city, we live on top of each other, and everyone seals themselves in at night. I thought I loved the pitch-black of it, you know? But after a short time, I gave myself to the vista, the storm watching over me as I slept. It was… amazing. I see why you love this place."

"You like the dress? It's lovely on you."

"Thank you. Yes, it's quite comfortable. The fabric is so luxurious. Was it your wife's?"

"Yes. Everything in your suite was hers. I'm glad it all fits you."

"Marcus… I must ask. There are few online photos I could find. I… did you choose me for this interview and ask me to stay overnight because of… how I look?"

"Why? Are you pretty? I hadn't noticed." I don't think my smile did much to break the tension in the room.

"When I first saw you interviewing Robert Andrews in London, I was captivated."

"I see."

"Yes. I admit that's what got me thinking of doing this interview, to meet you. I watched that video many times. I chose you because of your conversational style, passion for the truth and story, and honest reporting."

Okay, that was all true. If it weren't, I would still have chosen her.

"Shall we get back to it then?"

"Eat first. Then we'll walk the grounds, and you may ask as many questions as you like. It's a lovely day out there."

***

We walked the garden first, and her questions focused on the vegetables and how a science geek like me learned how to garden—the internet, of course. Through the open field, I saw a city girl in the wide-open countryside. The joy beamed from her face like a child who'd just learned to ride a bicycle—a new and wonderful freedom and exhilaration overwhelming her.

Then she remembered why she had come.

"We left off with you realizing your failure. You had invented time travel and could relive moments of the past in the… *overlap*, you called it. But you couldn't save Ellie, to stop what happened to her. Tell me about that moment."

"The second worst day of my life." I blinked hard to fight back the tears. They hadn't come in years. How had Jessica roused such emotion from the permafrost my soul had become? "You don't have your notebook."

After a chuckle, she stopped her steps and took my arm. "I only doodle on that thing. I have this amazing memory for words and stories. I never take notes beyond an occasional date or detail. You said you liked my conversational style… This is how I do it. When you're ready to talk about it, I'm ready to listen."

Who was this woman, this Jessica Matthews? I lost myself entirely to her charms. No one has ever affected me in this way. No one besides my Ellie until now. Now, in my old age.

For the first time since the police interrogation, I recounted the incident under the streetlight. Compassionate ears gave me full attention and sorrowful understanding. Impending tears glossed Jessica's eyes. We found ourselves on the walking path through a thick of trees to the south side of the house. I'd always trekked here alone and basked in the solace, convinced it was perfect. This exceeded that perfection by miles.

Arm-in-arm, we strolled in tranquility until we cleared the miniature forest into the field again. Audible growls from my stomach told us how close to lunchtime it had become. The sun had told me to head back. It must have been about one o'clock. I ignored its warning to stay in the moment. When Jessica agreed with my empty belly's request, we returned to the house and finished the tale of loss and heartache on the way.

Over the Cobb salads and herb-rubbed chicken, Jessica volunteered to tell her story of lost love. As hard as I found it to believe, she had been left behind by a man driven by his career to move on without her.

"So, you realized you couldn't save her. But you visited her in the overlap… didn't you?"

"A great many times, yes. I started with memories, constructing scenes with the AI in Transcend. The lack of realness failed me, failed her. When I stopped fighting the physics of time travel and its limitation of not altering the outcome, I repeatedly lost myself in the overlap."

"Which moments did you choose to relive? If… I may ask."

"Jessica, dear, I told you you may ask me anything. I chose many. When we first met, our first date, our wedding day. The first time we made love. I lived these events over and over again."

"And the day of… the day she died?"

My head hung low over the scraps of lunch remnants that clung to my plate. "Of course. I had to try. I said, 'physics be damned, I have to try.'"

"And every time you came out… she was still gone."

"No way to change the past. I knew this, of course, but stubbornly I tried… repeatedly."

"That must have been so difficult. I… I can't imagine the pain of reliving that."

"That's just it."

I stood, ready to resume the interview position in the study. Jessica followed, and I closed the wall to hide her ensuite as I poured my after-lunch scotch and handed her a bottle of water.

"You see, Jessica… I *could* stop it. I did stop it—every time. Then, we shared experiences that never happened but were as real as this conversation. As real as last night's storm and the meal we just enjoyed." I sipped my drink and held the glass up. "Like this scotch. As physical and real as anything. It, well, transcended Transcend. I lived it, felt it, smelled her, touched her, and made love to her. And those memories are as real as the ones that happened in normal-time."

"How many times did you go back?"

"More than I could count. Oh, the machine logged all my trips, but I deleted those after each go when Peter started on me for losing myself in the overlaps. He pushed me to make a commercially viable product out of it."

"And that's how you came up with *Vacations in Time?*"

"Peter's idea. His name. I suggested *Holidays in Time,* but Peter thought it was too British. He said Americans would think of actual holidays, like Christmas and such. Of course, he was correct. Still, I never cared for the name… or the business."

"It made you rich."

"I was already rich. It gave me more money to donate."

"Ellie's namesake foundation."

"So, Peter commercialized it. Soon, shops sprang up around the world full of my chambers ready to send travelers back to moments in their own lives."

"People stayed in there for various lengths of time. How long could they stay in an overlap?"

"Dear Jessica, those are two different things, staying in the machine and time in the overlap. We learned early on how time in the overlap moved more quickly than in real-time in the chamber. An average hour in normal-time saw close to a day in the overlap. Longer than that, we believed the brain wouldn't be able to process."

"The brain. You had some medical experts on the team. What was their role?"

"Research, at first. We dared not stay in the machine for more than a few minutes in normal-time until we understood how the brain would process the events in the overlap. Deep inside the temporal lobe, the hippocampus plays a central role in our ability to remember, imagine, and dream."

While I followed the medical research, it had been some time since I had to explain it. Jessica followed with eyes sharply focused on me.

"The thing about the old metaverse and *Transcend*... the brain stores those events as imagination and dreams. You come out with the memory, but it feels much like having watched a film or waking from a dream. You've been in *Transcend*, so you understand."

"Yes, exactly."

"Reality and imagination flow in different directions in the brain. The visual information from real events we experience that the eyes see flows *up* from the brain's occipital lobe to the parietal lobe. However, imagined images flow *down* from the parietal to the occipital."

"It's like a salmon swimming upstream."

"A simple analogy, but a good one. Only salmon get where they need to go."

"Unless a bear grabs it." Her radiating smile filled the room with warmth.

"Right. Our specialists explained how our brains are the bears. We construct new fictitious scenes activating the hippocampus, parahippocampal gyrus, retrosplenial cortices, posterior parietal cortices, and ventromedial prefrontal cortex."

"Got it. Maybe you could explain it so *my readers* will understand."

"Sorry. Years ago, studies showed certain parts of the brain were involved in forming *false* memories, and different parts of the brain were responsible for creating *true* memories. While progress has been made in merging these, trying to build real memories from the fictitious, this is military-grade stuff, and as far as I know, so far unsuccessful."

"Then, if I remember something as real, it *was* real. Imagination, dreams, even Transcend experiences, are stored as… false memories."

"Exactly. That's why *Vacations in Time* became such an international phenomenon. Being in the overlap created memories of real events."

"Then why did you shut it down?"

8 | The Limit

DAYS like this didn't come often for me. In fact, I hadn't had one in forty years. Staying in Jessica's presence required no effort, pretense, or awkwardness. Talking with her felt as natural as breathing. She had assumed, correctly, that I've had few friends in my long years of life. Ellie brought out something in me that no one else did. In her, I found a closeness I desperately wanted.

"Marcus? I think I lost you for a moment."

"I'm here. My mind doesn't always like to stay with me. It has that in common with most people."

"Really? You've been reclusive for most of your life, but your company is delightful. If you're back with me… I had asked why you shut down the vacation business when it had been so lucrative?"

"You must suspect it was the military contracts? Most reports speculated as much. No. In truth, we had licensed the machine to the military early on. They had no exclusivity clauses, only that we kept the technology strictly proprietary and only used it for the vacation business."

"I had heard the same, of course. I'm not fond of assumptions. I prefer to ask the source, and here I am… with you."

"Indeed. First, we discussed the limit on how long one can stay in the machine. This leads directly to why I shut down the business despite Peter's protests. That and the number of repeat trips to overlaps."

"Was there a limit on repeat trips? I've never heard that."

"Not exactly, but we're getting ahead. Only with the world's highest-ranking neuroscientists' assistance did we increase trips in time to more than a few minutes. Peter and I had been the only humans in the chamber at that point. Those few minutes gave me precious few hours with Ellie. Like an addictive drug, I craved more. And like an addict, I would have done anything to get another fix."

"How long did you stay in?"

"See, you ask the right questions, the smart questions. I was the first to stay for an hour. Officially. That gave me an entire day with Ellie."

"Officially?"

"That night, I worked late, as I always did, and was alone in the lab. I entered with an eight-hour timer and spent a week with my darling Ellie. I overlapped at dinner just before we walked home and insisted we take a cab. It was the first time I made *new* memories with her."

"And you were fine… obviously. Is that when you set a hard limit?"

"Fine, yes. Physically, I was fine. Having filled my bladder with coffee, water, and scotch, I wet myself in the chamber. And I emerged incredibly thirsty. I saw the need to control the body as it passed through normal-time in the chamber."

"The drugs and IV's?"

"Yes. We rushed those through the FDA and began human trials. I was the first to stay in for over a day. Two at first, then three."

"Each time living new experiences with Ellie?"

"Mostly. I relived a vacation she wanted, but where I insisted on a destination she hated. The second time, we went to Seychelles as she wished, not the South African Safari of my choosing. To redo that mistake and enjoy those weeks is a new, *real* memory—vivid to this day…"

"But for the entire run of your stores, you held to a hard two-day limit. What happened when you went beyond that?"

"The body felt the effects. Drugs kept me hydrated and pumped me full of nutrients. Tubes removed the waste. We noticed only a trace onset of atrophy at first, knowing the muscles took a couple of weeks or more to suffer from disuse."

Jessica doodled on her pad.

"May I see what you're drawing?"

"I have only a few interview rules, but no one sees my notes or doodles. Now, I'm curious about the effects on the body if atrophy wasn't the issue. What happened to you over three days?"

"This is where the medical jargon lost me, honestly. The best I understood is that with the mind so active, living weeks' worth of experiences in mere days took a toll as signals from the brain in the overlap reached the physical body in normal-time."

"What is the longest you stayed in?"

"Officially? Four days. Then, three days in the hospital to recover."

I crossed my legs and leaned back as Jessica fidgeted. The midday sunlight shone over her in a heavenly glow, and—from her shampoo or soap or a mental non-reality—the herbaceous scent of daisies swirled around me. Subtle yet alluring.

"There's that word again. What was the longest you stayed in the chamber *unofficially*?"

"Fifteen days."

"*Fifteen?*" In full reporter mode, she stood up to face me. The window's illumination caught the edges of her dress, Ellie's dress, outlining her shape. "How long was that in the overlap? Almost… a year?"

"More. No, your math was spot on. I found an unexpected anomaly in the overlap. The longer I stayed, the more time from the real world, normal-time, stretched."

"Why not sixteen days or seventeen? What made you stop at fifteen?"

"I had worked my way up. Four, five, six, and so on. I got to a point with the drugs and advanced treatments— and a medical monitoring team—I made it to seven without getting myself hospitalized."

"Seven is a stretch away from fifteen."

"A deprivation tank, modified, of course. In a synthetic… *amniotic* fluid, I made it to twelve days. In the fluid, the overlap stretched even further. I then decided to rid myself of anything of normal-time other than my body. No watch, no clothes, nothing."

"Somehow, being naked allowed you to stay longer?"

"It did. I'm sure you're aware of our Ultra Overlap packages where our clients entered similar, though more elegant, tanks to experience the greatest passage of jumped time."

"Of course. However, clients were allowed a max of two days in the chambers and tanks. Why?"

"Fifty-two hours, to be precise. It's what we, that is to say, the medical team, deemed safe. The Ultra clients experienced two and a half months in the overlap. Standard chamber clients a few weeks. Of course, these were expensive packages, even the standard. Most of our clients spent only a few hours in normal-time."

"Yes. I'm aware."

Something struck me in the certainty of her tone. Jessica sat, crossing her legs and doodling some more. I couldn't believe I hadn't asked this earlier.

"You've been in?"

"Hasn't almost everyone?"

"I'd be curious about what overlap you chose and for how long. And you must have been quite young. We closed shop over fifteen years ago."

"Let's save that for another time. I'm supposed to be interviewing you, remember? Tell me about the fifteen days and how many times you did it."

"Too many times. I had gotten the chemicals and the fluid to slow brain activity in my body to the point my fifteen days in the tank spanned fourteen to fifteen years in the overlap. And I relived that decade and a half many times."

"What did you do with those years?"

"We lived. We loved each other. We spent all our money on vacations and traveled the world together. Once we raised a family."

"Each time was pure bliss?"

Where did that question come from? Logical, I suppose. No, there was more to it. Through squinted, contemplative eyes, I examined the gentle seriousness on her face. "Not every time."

"What do you mean?"

"See, during the overlap, you can change things. I saved Ellie each time, and we lived those years together in most of the jumps I made." I poured myself a scotch and sipped liberally. "See, it was the same world. Politics and social issues happened the same, every jump. Just the way it happened in normal-time."

"What happened… to you?"

"I learned from experience to be more careful in researching the fifteen years I'd spend there. As you pointed out yesterday evening, I hid for those years in normal-time. I didn't follow the news. Ellie and I experienced a well-known plane crash I could have avoided. We were viciously attacked once, barely survived a mass shooting at a concert, and twice we were in horrific car accidents."

"Then what happened to you in the real world?"

"Those worlds *were* real. That was, at times, the problem. If I died, I woke before the timer. Once, I wished I *had* died. Ellie was taken from me, and I relived that pain in a new and horrifying way."

"And… you took your own life?"

Shame added weight to my chin, pulling it down to lower my head. "Yes."

9 | The Clients

SOBBING never described the effect of emotion on me. I'd shed tears and had not been a man afraid to admit that or let it show. Ellie thought it made me human when so much of my life made me less so in her eyes. I had no idea how Jessica Matthews would react. Undoubtedly, she'd seen much in her career and reported on disasters, mass murders, wars, and worse. My gaze out the window proved insufficient to hide the sadness behind my eyes.

A warmth touched my arm, and my cloudy vision found its source in Jessica's gentle touch. On her knees beside my chair, she looked upon me with such tenderness, one that my callous soul hadn't absorbed in decades. Yet I felt no virile desires rising to the surface. There was something… something else about her.

Although Jessica was a young, vibrant woman oozing muliebrity, and age hadn't wholly robbed me of the animal desires common to men—I enjoyed watching Samantha clean the house a little too much. However, that had been the extent of it for years. With Jessica—a much more striking creature than Samantha—this hit different chords within me. I had so little experience with women, with much of anyone for most of my life, that I couldn't quantify my current experience or its effect on me.

"Maybe, when you're ready, you could tell me about some of your clients."

"Yes. Who came to travel through time, their past, and why? Of course, our first 'clients' were members of our team. The corporate office had grown to over four hundred before we opened a single shop. Peter sent them worldwide to fill the first twenty stores, making it look like it was already mainstream."

"It worked. From your opening week, you had solid bookings until you closed. Two to three months was the average wait time for an appointment."

"We opened over a thousand stores and couldn't meet the demand. For many, Transcend became plan B or what they did in the interim while they waited for their slot in my machine."

"Your staff had to set the parameters for each client's jumps back in time. Did your system log the events and relived memories as Transcend does?"

"My machine is nothing like Transcend. That system requires much input and user detail as it must create simulated events from memory or fantasy. Our clients only had to supply an exact date and time. The machine didn't care where in the world they were for the overlap, what they did, or with whom."

I had Jessica's full attention. My pause widened her eyes.

"Remember, my machine doesn't recreate memories and build synthetic scenes. It sends people back to a moment in time to relive it. No, we didn't log the trips or ask the clients for details. Not at first."

"Interesting… You speak of your machine in the present tense though all reports said every chamber had been disassembled and all research and technical specifications destroyed."

It's clever how she caught my lapsus linguae. "Yes, that is true. And we never produced another chamber, not even for the military—which was a breach of contract, I add. Of course, I assume they still use the ones we supplied years ago."

"I do want to get to that in a bit. We know very little about the military contracts and how they used your machine. For now… I think there's much more to those early clients. Please tell me more about how they reacted to the overlap and how the business snowballed."

"We developed a thirty-minute safety and expectations program and required every first-timer to go through it and pass a brief quiz. Repeat customers did a ten-minute recap, no matter how often they entered a chamber."

"When you launched, the stores hadn't yet offered the Ultra experience, correct?"

"Again, excellent work on your research. Standard chambers only, from launch and for the first three years. Peter would have said it was his marketing genius, getting customers to return for a new experience while attracting a wealthier clientele."

"And what would *you* say?" Jessica smirked as if she'd known the answer.

"I forbade it. The fluid chambers weren't ready for mass production or safe for consumer use."

"That took you three years to perfect?"

"Perfect? I'd not say that about any of my work or of anyone else's, for that matter. No, that's how long I could stall Peter's ambition. It was ready and safe, just over eighteen months from store openings."

"Then why the delay?"

"Jessica, you've already learned more about me than anyone else on the planet. I've not spoken to my chef or housekeeper as much in over a decade as with you in these few hours. Why do *you* think I delayed?"

I toyed with her, testing the sharpness of that impressive mind. The pause provided the space to refill my tumbler, but I hadn't emptied it. Stimulating conversation didn't require the soothing liquid as much as a typical afternoon alone, with only my thoughts.

"You were the only one who used it. It was your special chamber, … your personal experience, not to be shared."

Such a clever one. Parts of me felt as exposed and known to her as years had done to me under Ellie's spell. What witchery did Jessica Matthews possess to have me so vulnerable in mere hours? I fidgeted at the discomfort not in my body; the one rattling the bones of my inner self, my soul, could not leave me still.

That darn squeak. Samantha's been telling me to have it fixed for years. 'Leather farts,' she called it when my chair pushed air through that little slit. The smile it drew on Jessica's lovely face made me glad I had ignored the nagging housekeeper.

"Sorry," I smirked sheepishly. "Must be the Cobb salad."

Her laughter made an exceptional afternoon even lovelier.

"Flatulence aside, did I get it right?"

"Oh yes. That you did… I admit…, it took me aback a pinch. That's why I got fidgety there. Please, I must know how you reached that conclusion."

"Because you've shut yourself off from the world doesn't mean you're all that complicated a person. You are narcissistic—brilliant, yes. Most brilliant people, in my experience, are narcissists."

"I'd say that comes with the job. Certain levels of brilliance and accomplishment require a healthy bit of narcissism. Wouldn't you agree?"

"I would. More than that… I think there's more to it. You created the device for personal reasons, not for commercialization, and Peter pilfered it, making it into a global sensation shared by billions."

"Intriguing. Please, go on."

"I was going to." A wink. When was the last time anyone shot *me* a playful wink? "I think you resented him for it. That's the real reason for the divide, the growing animosity between you. He took your work, your intimately private experience with Ellie, and made it… *commonplace.*"

Eerie how well she understood me. Perhaps I hid myself to keep others from seeing what was so readily apparent. What makes me tick, they say. Like anyone's heard a mechanical device—a clock, watch, anything—*tick* in ages.

"The extended time from the fluid in the chamber, *your* chamber, was yours and yours alone."

The first pop drew Jessica's shoulders in and rounded her eyes. A foolish instinct; I didn't know why I clapped just there. Such an act always comes off as sarcastic or… *oh no*… condescending.

"Sorry. I don't know why I did that. I'm truly impressed. You are indeed correct. My failure that time—so many so-called successes sprouted from my greatest fail-ures—was telling Peter about the fluid and its effects."

"Still, you stayed in the fluid for fifteen days, while your clients got only fifty-two hours."

"True. I'd never considered it a consolation, something uniquely my own after the Ultra experience launched. Thank you for that perspective, Jessica."

"Happy to help."

10 | The Military

LIFE on Earth had been obliterated by nuclear detonations with enough destructive force to wipe out all living organisms on the planet a dozen times over. And they did it repeatedly. Politicians and generals debated the results on the other side of the overlaps.

"Even the cockroaches died, despite what you may have heard postulated. Each time they did it, they'd been able to save only a handful of humans in nuclear bunkers. And these would have to stay there for generations until the nuclear winter eased into a springtime nightmare on the surface."

"As I understand it, joint leaders from all nuclear powers engaged in such exercises, replaying scenarios of global thermonuclear war and trying to manipulate its outcomes."

"Correct. Of course, this did not happen immediately. No, our illustrious leaders first exhausted all possibilities of *winning* such a conflict. Only when the inevitable global devastation was undeniable did they invite leaders of the seven nuclear power states to participate."

"And your invention led the world to the completely denuclearized planet we enjoy today."

"The most uncommon thing in our world, common sense, finally kicked in. The arms race was one no one would win, and no governing power in their right mind would dare launch the first nuke, knowing it would have only one conclusion, no matter how they played it out."

"You saved the world. Without your invention to make what was so obvious to us all finally penetrate those stubborn, self-pleasing politicians' closed minds… we'd all be gone by now."

"My dear, 'saved the world' is a bit too grandiose, even for me to concede. But I am grateful my invention helped bring them to their senses. Yes, I'm extremely grateful for this."

"We all are. And that's the first thing that search engines display for your name. You must scroll a bit to find the articles on *Vacations in Time* and more… personal discussions."

"But not for poor Peter, eh?"

"I think you know as well as I; his suicide always comes up first, no matter the search engine."

"A shame, really, to reduce his legacy to that. What a name his boys have inherited."

"The sins of the father, as you said." Jessica paused contemplatively as if surprised by her own words. "But the military did much more than that with your device, didn't they?"

I gave the question a moment but not to play with the lovely reporter. I had to consider her question in the context of her words and my earlier replies.

"We enjoy the denuclearized world my invention created. You said that." She nodded. "But we don't enjoy peace, do we?"

"No. Far from it. There continue to be wars and weapons of mass destruction used. Just not… nuclear."

"Exactly. We've reverted to killing each other in more animalistic ways. Like I said yesterday, prehistoric human mentality."

"Only, we're not hitting each other over the head with clubs."

"Exactly." She followed so well as if she knew my train of thought as my mind loaded its cargo. "We use tanks, bombs, submarines, and airplanes, same as before. While we may not be able to destroy all life on earth in a single go any longer, the body counts continue to grow."

"And somehow your invention plays into that count?"

"Now you see why I said I wasn't worthy of the honor so many would afford me. My machine has been, and likely still is, used to train soldiers in new forms of combat. The United States of America and Britain—what a name they chose when the US and UK unified—can run test conflicts, incursions, attacks, and full-scale wars in an overlap over and over until they find the perfect strategy, timing, approach, to win."

"And now they rule more than half the world."

"Much more if you go by population rather than geography. Annexing China doubled its governed populace. And massively increased its wealth."

"After the shared nuclear war overlaps, the USAB retained exclusive rights to your machine?"

"Yes. But that added a complex layer to our client vetting, leading to the government ordering our withdrawal from several countries to protect the technology."

"I heard they tried to shut down the entire operation."

"If not for Peter and his tenacity, more his generous campaign contributions, they would have. We climbed a mountain of paperwork and agreed to regulatory agents assigned to each location to stay in business."

"I think this was another area where you and he didn't see eye to eye."

"Most astute, Jessica. As I've said, the money was never important to me. My fortune came from royalties off that original network backbone project. I've donated every cent from my machine, including all proceeds from that business. Mine, of course, not Peter's."

"Of course." When Jessica raised the corner of her lips, I saw Ellie's sly smirk. She always caught me when I tried to be self-righteous—an all too pretentious act, as she knew well. "How did you feel having government regulatory agents in your shops?"

"I couldn't have cared less. I left that to Peter. I had never stepped foot into any of our stores."

"Earlier, you said the in-chamber limit and the government contracts eventually led to the stores being closed and the machines dismantled. How did that transpire?"

"Those are separate but related points. Let me start by saying we supplied the military with advanced versions of Ultra's deprivation tanks. They sent people in for fourteen days at a stretch. They played their war games to see the long-range effects, seeing the consequences to nearly fourteen years in the future."

"I thought you were the only one to stay in that long."

"*Officially.*" She reciprocated my smirk with a broad smile full of teeth. "And I was the only one ever to do fifteen days. That was true. But their extended time taught us much more than my time in the tank. After all, I limited my world scope to what Ellie and I experienced."

"Taught you what, exactly?"

"What someone did in an overlap... it had consequences."

"But nothing had changed when they came out. Those worlds, the overlap, as real as they seemed, were only real to the traveler. Or so you said."

"And so I believed. And yes, nothing in the real world changed when the traveler exited the chamber, as I proved repeatedly trying to save my Ellie. But in there, in a world as real as this one, though temporary, the traveler's actions caused suffering and hardships."

"What did that matter? I get that an overlap feels real, as much a reality as normal-time. But in the end… wasn't it just a fantasy world—not real in any *physical* sense?"

"Yes, yes. You understand perfectly. If you've been in, maybe you can try to relate. You live your experience, and you feel everything as in normal-time, in the real world. But what if you saw someone hurt, a child injured, a natural disaster wiping out thousands, a terrorist attack? You'd experience that pain, the grief it brings, the same as if it happened in the real world."

"I get that, Marcus. That means it stays with you or the traveler. As real to you as experiencing it in the real world. I'd imagine then, once a traveler exits the machine, they realize it didn't happen."

"Remember what I said about the working of the brain when it comes to memories, real versus fantasy? What makes my machine so different from Transcend."

Jessica leaned forward with a stern stare focused on my paled face. "Yes."

"*You* don't come out of the machine unaffected by the experience." I sipped the scotch I'd almost forgotten between my fingers. "To the traveler, it was authentic."

I thought I'd lost her momentarily as she appeared to slip into isolation into her own contemplation, gazing around me to stare through the wide glass, mentally gliding over the open field.

"Oh. And those soldiers and politicians? They lived through horrific experiences in the overlaps."

"Madness. Depression. Suicides. My invention that saved the world… ruined plenty of lives along the way. Destroyed families. Broke people's hearts. Killed people."

"You can't blame yourself for how people used your invention."

"No? It's nothing new. Nobel, Einstein, Oppenheimer. I leaned upon the same crutch. My invention would ensure peace, advance science for the benefit of humankind, and end wars. Blah, blah, blah. As with others before me, that crutch crumbled beneath me."

11 | The Consequences

FILLING nearly the entirety of the wall beside my desk, the vista beyond the glass always calmed me. I stared into the nothingness it showed me today as Jessica used the restroom—a welcome break from the conversation. Though heavy, I found it stimulating parts of my mind and soul that had been dormant for too long before yesterday evening. Of all my failures, I pondered if social isolationism could be my most significant.

Somber eyes filled with a ray of anticipation were watching Jessica Matthews saunter into the study from the small hall connecting it to the dining room. She looked at home like she'd always been here with me. A realism beyond an overlap overwhelmed me at that moment. Self-interestedly, I played with this woman's ambition, her thirst for the exclusive exposé, the first and all-informative interview with the reclusive inventor of *Vacations in Time*.

I could have been in *trænSɛnd* with a virtualized version of her floating around me. No, this experience had a realism that the fantasy world lacked. I could feel the warmth in her smile on my skin as she sat beside me. Like an overlap, only this wouldn't vanish when I emerged from the tank.

There is no tank. This is real.

"Sorry. I guess I drank more water than I realized."

"No worries. I have all day." I smiled, not wanting this to end. I did indeed have all day. All week. The rest of my days, in fact.

"I could tell we hit a nerve just then, on the aftereffects of your machine on its travelers. I'm sorry for dredging that up."

"No. It was I who did the dredging, my dear. It's good to get this off my chest finally. The guilt lays thicker over it than the curly gray hairs." A reach for a chuckle came out as a half cough.

"Consequences of a traveler's overlap rest squarely on the traveler. I think you went a little too hard on yourself."

"And the judge agreed. Jessica, there have been other lawsuits, though never publicized. Each settled quietly between Peter's legal team and the claimants. Financially acceptable for the cost of doing business, as Peter repeatedly said. I didn't weigh the cost in dollars."

"How many lawsuits? What happened to the travelers?"

"Peter tried to keep many from me, seeing how they tore me to shreds each time. I know of twenty-two, but I'm sure there were more."

"All settled out of court?"

"All left people—the traveler or their family—rich. And quiet."

A dense silence filled the room for the first time since Jessica's arrival. I considered her face, studying the outline of her jaw, the focus in her eyes. Focused not on me or any physical object in her sight, she looked through me into her mind, yet I felt her peeling the layers of my flesh and seeing the exposed bone. A shame of nakedness washed over me, the reporter looking in on me with no blur filter.

"Marcus, you never said you wished to speak off the record. Are you sure you want this included in the interview?"

"Peter is gone. The business has been closed for well over a decade. We've nothing to lose; no more need for the silent charade. People loved us, willingly forked over tons of their hard-earned cash for a chance to experience the machine, their *vacation in time*." I laced those last words with contempt as I vomited them out of my throat.

"I hear lots of regrets in less-than-subtle undertones."

"As I've said, I merit no respect for being a clever inventor. People loved us and loved the experience of traveling into an overlap. Some became addicted, as I did. And for some, we ruined their lives."

"The madness, depression, suicides, you spoke of… These weren't limited to military use, were they?"

"Again, most perceptive, young lady. Some of our private clients suffered the same ill effects. They came out changed people, some screwed up in the head."

"Why? How? I thought most relived joyous times in their past. What happened to them?"

"Some did, yes, many. Then, the harsh realities of life in normal-time set in, harming some under the weight of real-life problems and anxiety. Some lost it when told they had to wait three months for another 'fix'. We had a couple of violent episodes in our stores."

"Those were reported, but as random acts of violence or terrorism. Now I'm getting they weren't so random."

"Not at all. Our *happy*"—set in air quotes—"customers' way of saying, 'thanks for ruining my life.'"

"I see. And what of those who didn't shoot up the place?"

"The lawsuits, as I mentioned. However, the wealthier ones continued, paying their way handsomely through the waiting list—addicts like me getting their next fix. We had our medical team devise a withdrawal treatment. Few accepted admittance into the free program, and those who did often crashed into depression."

"Surely, *they* are to blame for how they used the machine. Earlier, you said *initially* you didn't track where people went or what they did."

"Does nothing get by you?" A glimmer in her eye said nothing did. "Only as a necessary precaution and means to understand how to prevent our clients from crashing or suffering the after-effects of an overlap."

"I'll go out on a limb here, though I'm fairly sure of the answer… The clients weren't made aware of this necessary precaution, were they?"

"It was a clear violation of our client privacy agreement."

"And a federal offense." Jessica could say much in a few words. I gathered she understood my motivations in why I'd risk such a breach.

"That too."

"There's more. You spoke earlier of the consequences to others *in* the overlap, the effects on them, though temporary and gone once the traveler's journey ended. You were concerned about that. What I don't understand is why."

"It's what some of our clients were doing in there."

12 | The Diva

"MIND you, most of our clients had perfectly honorable travels. Many experience review questionnaires included a summary of their overlap—completely voluntary. Stories of reliving love affairs, redoing lost moments with loved ones, parents revisiting the childhood of their grown offspring."

Jessica liked hearing about this, I could tell. Her face shone where earlier thoughts of the troubles the machine caused looked to have unsettled her.

"We had several professional athletes reliving their glory days. One case, heartbreakingly beautiful in its sentiment, was Melody Buonavoce." A puzzled look. Jessica was young, but I'd have thought everyone had at least heard of one of the most famous singers of the last half-century. "You don't know her?"

"Not that I recall."

"*The Way You Love Me. Silently Soulful. Midnight Melody.*" Blank looks on each. "You've not heard any of these songs?"

"Perhaps if I heard them, I'd recognize them. I'm not into much music outside of new-age jazz."

"Now that's surprising. Majel, play *Silently Soulful* by Melody Buonavoce… This is my favorite."

I watched Jessica absorb the music as the barely audible introduction of wind instruments graduated into notes as the piano joined the harmony. The slow build into the melody churned like a deep hunger, salivating the earbuds until satiated by an auditory explosion of drums, piano crescendo, and trumpet blasts. Powerful. Then Melody's angelic vocals…

"You've heard this one, I'm sure. That voice."

"Yes, now that you've played it. Of course. Her vocals are pitch-perfect. So… what's her overlap story?"

A raised finger asked her to hold the questions until the song finished. I closed my eyes and leaned back to soak in the treble and feel the bass. The soothing soul in that voice invariably moved me.

"Okay. You must have heard of her throat cancer, which ended her tragically short career. She was a holdout, one of the last smokers. I think she sucked down the last of the world's supply of cigarettes."

"How sad."

"My machine gave her her voice back. She went in once a month for over a year to perform her final concert to fifty thousand adoring fans. I wished then I could travel with her, experience that moment."

"That wasn't possible. *Right?*"

"Correct… *Officially.*"

"That word again. I should expect the unofficial by now."

"I promised you an exclusive. What have I got to lose? *Unofficially…* I took years of data from our neuroscience team, some bits from the Transcend code, and worked with the readings from my machine's scanner to find a way to observe someone's overlap. Sort of."

"Unofficially. Sort of. And we're still on the record. Explain what you did and how it worked."

"We never could see, hear, or feel what happened in an overlap. That was always only the traveler's sole experience. We extrapolated enough data to create a transcend construct, basic shapes like the archaic original metaverse at best."

"So, you *did see* a representation of what they did. That was a massive violation of privacy."

"And why we hardly ever used it."

"Almost. You and your teasing words."

She had me. I was enjoying the teasing, the titillating of her inquiring nature. I think she read the satisfaction from my face like words on her tablet.

"You're right, Jessica. I love to tease, to bait you until you bite. I developed the invasion—that's what I called it—to see if we could offer shared overlaps as a new customer offering. Peter figured we'd triple our already colossal profits."

"I've seen nothing on that. Not a single leaked detail you were even trying that."

"No, of course, we never shared that. Only Peter and I knew we could do it."

"But it was rubbish. The experience so limited you never offered it."

"Exactly. I hoped, after getting Melody's permission, of course, to watch one of her encore performances. She'd sing for three hours, with only a few little breaks, while the orchestra performed instrumentals. She was an amazing performer, and I never saw her live."

"Why not go to her show in one of your own overlaps?"

"We did. Ellie and me. A few times. But I wanted to experience it with her, returning and giving it her all, knowing it was her last performance. I thought it would be more special."

"But you saw cartoon versions of people without sound."

"Shapes more than cartoon people. And no audio, no sensory input beyond the nondistinctive visual images my machine could form into a transcend projection."

"Another failure. I'm guessing Peter never found a way to make it into a success."

"No. I did. Well, sort of. I found a use for it after all." An overwhelming demand to justify myself washed through me as a novel sensation. I always figured my intelligence and money excluded me from such a lowly action. ligence and money excluded me from such a lowly action.

"No, Jessica, my dear. While I found a use for it, I'd not dare call it a success."

The reporter's piercing eyes caught a glimmer of afternoon sunlight reflected off the metal window frame. Perhaps the leadings of my teasing started wearing on her nerves. We'd spent an entire evening and most of the second day together when she'd come for a one-hour chat. It was time to give her what she came for.

"Go on, Marcus. Just tell the story; no more dangling your bait. What use did you find for this *invasion* into people's overlaps?"

"Remember that I said most of our clients used their trips for a wholesome redo of a key moment in their lives. Either to experience that moment of bliss over again or to improve it, take a different course, and live new experiences."

"Of course, as you did many times. I know positive customer testimonials flooded the internet, and your Trustpilot ratings were always a solid five out of five up until you closed."

"Right." Again, I teased a word. "I'm sorry. I said *most* of our clients. As I told you, we had a strict screening, mostly for foreign government spies. It also caught some we suspected of wanting to go back for more nefarious purposes."

"Like what?"

My hand felt the emptiness of the tumbler I had set down without realizing I'd done it. I hadn't even finished my after-lunch scotch. I lifted and fumbled the crystal glass but lost the thirst for the aged liquid gold it held. A temporary sensation, I assure you, to build the tension for what I didn't relish discussing. Not for any desire for secrecy—that had long since faded.

"A few, some more heinous than others. Let me backtrack a bit to those few cases—and they were few—of post-overlap suicides."

"You said those were from people's experiences in the overlap driving them to depression."

"For some, yes, that happened. But I should tell you about Henry Shorter."

"A suicide? But not from depression."

"Oh, I'm not qualified to judge his mental state. I'd think anyone who'd taken their life likely had some problems they failed to get help to rectify. With all our advances in medicine and neuroscience, we still have such high rates worldwide. Sorry, I digressed. This topic…"

"And you took your own life once. In an overlap. If you had some mental distress in there, don't you think it reflects your condition out here, in normal-time?"

I let out a prolonged exhale. "Jessica… I wish not to degrade the situation of the many persons inflicted with mental health issues. I was a coward who couldn't live without my Ellie, not again. And I knew I'd wake up in normal-time."

"Point taken, Marcus. Please go on."

13 | The Lost Soul

WHY was I going down this road? Jessica, the sweet and compassionate listener, the reporter, Miss Jessica Matthews, who came for previously masked details, some insight into me—the man behind the cloak, the great Marcus Hollister, inventor of 'time travel.' The mention of Henry's name made my bones cold and achy.

I never met him.

"I don't recall why we picked him to check. We hadn't used the invasion on anyone besides Peter and myself. I never asked Miss Buonavoce since I knew it wouldn't work. Not for the experience I wanted, anyway."

"He ticked a box of some kind on the screening?"

"Yes, yes, that's it. Not for anything about Henry, but for the repetition of his travels."

"He was wealthy, then? You said only those who could buy their way to the front of the line got to go so often."

"You do listen well. Impressive with no notes. Henry was clever. We had about a three to three-and-a-half month wait in the… Chicago, I think it was… yes, in that store. He had booked several trips four months ahead, five in a single month. We didn't recommend more than one a week but hadn't forbidden it yet."

"You became suspicious of that, checked him out."

"Yes. His initial prescreening showed signs of irrational thought patterns. Again, we were not there to diagnose people, and the medical team's job was to ensure physical health above all, as we never allowed people in the chamber long enough to come close to mental strain."

"And this Henry Shorter, when did you use the invasion?"

"On his fourth trip. You see, the first three had all ended early."

"Meaning… he died in each of the overlaps."

"Exactly. Not common. I monitored him myself, though he never knew or spoke with me. Using the logs from his previous trips, I compared what I saw to the mental patterns recorded."

"You could tell what he was doing in his overlaps?"

"I could. As I said, the images were blurred and not very distinct." A prolonged pause drew the young woman's well-proportioned face closer in a forward lean.

"And?"

"I saw him try to kill himself repeatedly. Eventually, he succeeded and woke up."

"Then what? I mean, what could you do with someone like that?"

"Our medical staff offered him help. They called the suicide prevention hotline and arranged a psychological evaluation. One of our nurses escorted him to the hospital. I checked in on him shortly after."

"This sounds like it's leading to a happy conclusion, if not for your apprehension in starting the story."

"I listened in on his session and understood how disturbed the man had been. He used his overlaps to... practice the most effective way to die. And he never received the proper help he needed. This was before the latest USAB medical care reform. I offered to pay all his expenses. The best care, I insisted."

"Wait. I mean, that was kind of you, really. But paying for Henry's treatments… they let you listen in to his sessions?"

"*Let* is an interpretable implication of their level of co-operation. I inferred that as Henry's surrogate care-provider, or funder, I should be able to know what I was paying for. So, I took it upon myself to listen."

"And you wonder why rich people have such a reputation."

"No. I know exactly why. And people are a hundred percent correct. We are not to be idolized. I've made that clear to you a few times already."

"You have."

"Good. Back to poor Henry. You know, he had a rather good life—it seemed. His wife stayed by his side, loyal and loving. He had a decent job she said he enjoyed. They had recently gone on a dream vacation, and he had taken up photography to document it."

"Of course, we know depression doesn't mean being sad or having a miserable life."

"Yes, of course. And *seeing* that… it's so much more than knowing it. In Henry, I started to understand, but I think none of us truly can. Not completely."

"He was getting treatment, had support, and the best care. He still ended his life, though?"

"He did."

"And his wife?"

"Devastated, of course. The overwhelming feelings of guilt. I flew to Chicago to meet her, and we talked many times during Henry's treatment. I met with her once *after*. That visit… had unintended consequences."

"A lawsuit?"

"No. Not this time. It's… I just… we were… both weak."

"You slept with her? Right after her husband's suicide? *Marcus!*"

"I know, I know. We were weak, as I said. For her, it was a one-time release, something she needed but never intended to follow up."

"You had feelings for her."

With glazed-over eyes holding in the tears, I could only nod affirmatively.

"It was something else. Something more." The astute, youthful reporter with a wisdom beyond her years studied my face. "What really bothered you wasn't succumbing to the flesh in an emotional collapse. It, it was… *Ellie*."

It became impossible to hold back the sobbing, my eyelids a flimsy dam unable to contain the torrent behind them. I squeaked out a noise resembling a yes and cradled my face in my palms.

A warmth surrounded me, stretched across my back to reach my shoulder—another calming sensation on my arm. Remorseful eyes found Jessica leaning over me, holding me. Me, this old fool, broken and not the man the world believed me to be. *Why is she so compassionate and gentle towards me? Is this the human interaction I've shielded myself from all these years?*

I experienced the consolation of a caring companion.

"It's okay. You were still grieving yourself. I can't imagine the emotional weight of such a moment on you… or on Henry's wife."

A firm hold lifted my chin, and my jaw lay cradled in Jessica's understanding hand.

"Marcus… you were *not* unfaithful to Ellie."

14 | The County Clerk

A WRECK of a puny figure, a pitiful waste of a life, stared at me from the mirror. *Look at yourself. Face a mess, eyes reddened, babbling with words still unable to form in your mouth because you fell apart in front of the first guest you've entertained in over a decade. Guest. As if she were here as a friend to see me. No. The reporter, here for the story, had to calm me down so she could get it.*

Old clown. Pathetic. How did I think this would go?

Red heat filled my cheeks, evaporating the water from my scleras. That's more me, the man I recognize. Anger came naturally and most often focused inward. Just what all that was back there, I didn't know. I used the toilet, washed my hands and face, and yearned for a scotch.

Me.

The full-figured—I'd not say fat in an honest apprais-al—man of stature filled the reflection over the sink and said he was ready to get back in there and tell his story. I irritated myself when I thought in the third person.

Jessica returned from the kitchen with hands clench-ing a white and blue ceramic mug. A distortion blurred her face as the steam rose from her herbal infusion held up to her nose. Part of me found satisfaction in her contentment, her comfort in helping herself to make herself at home.

She'd be gone soon.

Jessica Matthews would soon leave with the story of her career. *She will leave me.* It will make her career, hoist-ing her from the dregs of online video journalism to the mainstream—instant fame. *She'll be gone, and I'll be here alone. Nothing new for me.*

"I'm glad you made yourself at home. Is it too cold in here?"

"A little, but I'm fine. If you don't mind, I'll use this blanket again."

"Of course. Anything you like."

With the fuzzy red throw blanket fitted over her shoul-ders, Jessica lifted her cup, blew gentle ripples over the pip-ing-hot liquid, and inhaled a sip. *She slurps her tea as my Ellie does. Did.* I poured myself a Lagavulin and downed a sip after it swirled over my tongue, my tastebuds dancing in the full array of fruity-sherry notes and smoky vanilla flavors.

Her voice carried in waves of lavender-scented air as soothing as a summer breeze. "Now, you said *people's* experiences—I think there are more stories about your clients. Something mushroomed, motivating you to shut the whole operation down."

"Indeed. Let me tell you about the county clerk. I'm sorry, I'd say old age has taken the woman's name from my mind, but you'd see through that charade. I never bothered to know it. What I needed to know was how she used my machine."

"More nefariousness, I assume."

"Unfortunately. You're too young to recall this... A good researcher, however. Let me test that a bit." I fell back to my teasing ways. The burden of the last memory lifted—no, I think *buried* would be the better word. "Do you know the meaning of *going postal?*"

That intrigued her. I could see she had no idea. "Postal... That's, yes, how people used to send things. By post."

"Good. Sadly, a reputation of disgruntled employees escalating to acts of workplace violence traced back, at least in rumor, to incidents at post offices. A trend that caught on, as trends do."

"*Trend.* You are indeed a cynical man."

"You should have seen the security we had in our office. Our private militia and the highest tech scanners to get into the building."

"Your next client, the story, it's about workplace violence?"

"A massacre. One of the worst mass killings this side of the USAB, and our side's have always been worse than on that soggy little island we annexed."

"We. You've never been political. Have you?"

"Simple geography, my dear. This side of the Atlantic is *we* because we are physically here. No, I left the political games to Peter, never cared for it myself."

"How did your machine connect to the worst workplace killing in USAB history?"

"You've been to a government office, yes? DMV, tax office, document clerk?" Her nod meant I had her with me. "This lady worked in the County Clerk's office. And let me tell you, as much as it drives you mad to be in one of those offices as a customer, citizen, whatever. Imagine how working in there eight hours daily, day after day, must eat away at your humanity."

"Sounds like you're justifying an incident of workplace violence and mass murder."

"Not at all. I think… it helps to understand why things happen. We can't ever hope to stop something we don't understand. See, legislatures, law enforcers, judges, jailers… all treat the symptoms. The *why* matters. Why do people do the things they do? Without that, we're in a never-ending whirlpool."

"You have a point."

"And, as you may have guessed, our shooter spent some time in her overlaps practicing and racking up the body count before she did it for real."

"I thought those were usually impulsive events. A snap, and someone goes off. This was premeditated, and to kill the most people possible?"

"Seemed so. I saw the indistinguishable blob people in her replayed overlaps. Each time she went in and tried it, she positioned herself and shot with different guns in ways that altered the count until she reached forty-two."

"Forty-two. How awful. Those poor people—their families."

"Seventy-nine. In normal-time, she made it to seventy-nine before a cop took her down."

"I imagine a lawsuit with families of victims as joint plaintiffs. Not so good for business… No… your business never suffered. You said… *Oh*, no one knew about the invasions, so no one knew about the shooter's overlaps."

"You're catching on. I can see you're going to be a rising media star. Not only because I've granted you this exclusive. You've got what it takes to do anything you wish. If I were still a working man, I'd offer anything you asked to get you to work for me."

"Well, you have a house to clean and food to cook."

Her smile said she joked there, but my mind fluttered with images of having her around full-time.

"And this no-name woman, the shooter. They took her down. You mean killed her?"

"No. They wanted her alive. I'm not the only one who knows we must understand the why. They had her down, about to close in on her, when she held the semi-automatic over her chest, barrel tip pressed into her chin, and took the *why* out of the equation."

15 | The Jilted Lover

NATURE teaches us that the female of the species is most often the more aggressive, violent, and even murderous. I dabbled in biology for a few months between semesters and learned of many species with females who eat the males, some directly after mating. Some of the barbarism in nature made humanity appear tame by comparison.

I figured Jessica knew that, so I spared her the monologue. I recounted some genuinely touching stories of lost loves reunited in the overlap or high school sweethearts redoing that moment they broke up and seeing where life took them together. I was far from alone in my quest to relive special moments or create new ones with a deceased spouse or partner. We started giving anniversary discounts for those.

Peter wanted to call it the Marcus Hollister Memorial Anniversary Special, but I wanted my name distanced from the financial aspects of my invention. It was too long anyway. I think he ended up calling it the Blue Night Anniversary Package or something like that. He sold a bunch of those. *That,* I remember clearly.

"Adam Solomon. Any woman would have considered themselves lucky to have him. He was the total package but in all the good ways. Handsome as any celebrity actor or model, yet grounded. He had a successful career, many friends, was loved by all and did well for himself. Nicest guy, too. I knew him."

"He worked for you?"

"How'd you know that? We never released any info on him."

"You had few friends, if any. You mentioned work colleagues. I think you called them all sycophantic. So, if you knew this guy, he must have worked for the company."

"He did." Perfect cheekbones under those full chestnut locks, excellent form, such a mind—all with a delightful personality full of kindness and compassion. No, forget Adam. The luckiest person alive is the one who'd have Jessica Matthews. "Clever. And he did very well for himself."

"Married?"

"Wasn't the type. Oh, but not a playboy." I had to reply to the raised eyebrow, pushing her assumption about Adam across the space between us. "When he found the right one, he latched on with tenacious loyalty."

"You knew him that well."

"Everyone did. And his partner, Lanisha, offered nothing but praise for him as well. Anyone could tell it was genuine. He, too, was over the moon for her and never stopped talking about her. Showered her with gifts and affection."

"Sounds like a fairytale love story. But with *you* telling it, I'm bracing for the fall into the Shakespearean tragedy abyss."

"Right again. They were great for a while, a few years. Lanisha worked with us, too, but in a different department. One day, she dumped him without warning. Have you ever seen a man heartbroken and so completely deflated he ached for death's release?"

Pensively, she looked up from the notepad she hadn't scribbled on in some time and speared me with her gaze. "Marcus, I've been with you nearly twenty-four hours now."

"Fair enough. That was Adam, too. Maybe that's why he's the only one I almost got along with in those few years between my hermitages."

"That tracks."

"Can't argue that. Also, like me, Adam withdrew and spent more time in the office."

"He worked on the machine?"

"No. That was always a one-person operation. No one else ever knew how it functioned or how to copy my work. Adam was a developer and worked on the commercial units' software. Like all employees, he had access to the machines we had in Peter's lavish corporate headquarters building."

"He started using it a lot after Lanisha left?"

"Left *him*. She continued working one floor below him. That tortured him. I think… it may have been easier losing someone, I mean factually losing them, as I did."

"Perhaps. Both have vastly different coping mechanisms."

Jessica spoke not from speculation but from experience. She had mentioned that one love was insane enough to have left her. Who else had she lost?

"Indeed. And yes, Adam lost himself in the machine, as I had. His frequency worried me, but he kept to set limits. He said the only way out of his devastation, to feel whole, was in an overlap, reliving the best moments with Lanisha."

"And you could relate."

"Of course."

"You gave him slack, didn't you?"

Head down, chin to my breastbone, I stared at my lap, at nothing. "I did. His time in increased as did his frequency of trips."

"Marcus, what happened? What did he do?"

Somber melodies played the strings of my heart at a haunting timbre, silencing those of Henry and his wife.

"He killed her. Horribly."

"He used his overlaps to… practice?"

"A disturbing trend, I know. We should have anticipated it; *I should have*. The almighty dollar blinded Peter. I should have known, taken precautions."

"You're a brilliant man, Marcus. No one can foresee every possible outcome or consequence. Not even you."

"Your pacification is appreciated, Jessica. I mean that. I don't deserve it. It's so clear to me now as it should have been then. After the first time, two or three times, I still hadn't seen it—refused to see it."

"You used the intrusion on his trips to see his overlaps. Did you try to stop him?"

"Again, you see things so clearly. You'd have seen this if you were with me then as now. You would have warned me. Ellie would have warned me."

"You can't be sure of what can only be speculated. You're being too hard on yourself."

"Not hard enough. I acted too late. I saw him practicing. I saw him butchering that poor girl… *over and over, over and over* again. Thank the ghosts in the machine. The detail wasn't there."

"You said you tried to stop him. Marcus, you tried."

Such softness, such understanding.

Undeserved.

"I tried. I deduced Adam meant to kill her in the office. He'd asked her to meet him after work for a coffee in the breakroom after everyone had gone. She accepted every time. He'd have a machete or an ax or some blunt instrument. The pure animalistic rage he'd unleash upon her body."

"Did you… Did you think Adam was getting that rage out of his system in the overlaps?"

"That's it. That's it exactly." Cracks peeled my words like painted wood left under the sun. "I hoped so, anyway. But I kept an eye on him. And, well, he invited her for that coffee."

"You were there? Called the police? What did you do?" The anxiety in her voice sat her on the edge of the sofa's cushion.

"I went, *alone,* to stop him. Only later did I learn he dropped me hints in his last overlap, knowing I was often the last person in the building, and I must have tried to stop him. He was ready for me. He knocked me over the head and locked me in a storeroom. I… I heard… *it, the whole thing.* That girl's screams, the… the… *terrible* noises. Her deafening bellows, pleading for mercy over his ravenous and insensible shouts."

Numbness stiffened my bones and hardened my flesh. Now, in the memory, as in that storeroom, I leaned over Ellie, brushed a lock of hair behind her ear, and watched her life force drain from her.

16 | The Breaking Point

AFTER providing the means for a suicidal man in need of care to enact his goal most efficiently, training someone to perfect the art of mass killing, failing to prevent the brutal murder of a lovely young woman, and witnessing—auditorily only, if I can be thankful for anything—her slaughter, you might think I'd have passed the breaking point. No, unfortunately, it took more than that.

When more than that came, I nearly lost what remained of myself.

"So, you see, my dear Jessica, while illegal and… of course, unethical, we saw the need to increase our monitoring. We needed to work against such insidious use of the machine to keep the business operating."

"You didn't care to—keep the stores and company going, I mean."

"Peter's determination. His greed and lust for fame and prominence. Did you know he had every magazine cover he ever appeared on framed in gold and protected under glass like they were the *Mona Lisa*? I never cared for that one. More a Van Gogh fan myself."

"I saw the print of *Café Terrace at Night* in the dining room."

"My favorite. And not a print." I dropped that to see her expression change. I asked her not to respect me, but a healthy bit of awe couldn't hurt. It gleamed off a face full of wonder.

"So, *you do* indulge a little with all that money."

"Such a lovely smile. I thought it and… I hope it doesn't bother you that I've said it. I find your company delightful and am pleased you accepted the offer to interview me. And I am truly sorry that I must remove that smile from you again."

"Another nefarious case?"

"The one that pushed me to the breaking point. After… *that*, I couldn't let it keep going. What's worse, perhaps, yes… I think so… is not knowing how many more there were. We caught only the one."

The face so full of life and contagious energy paled in anticipation. I'd shared such horrors already. What might she have imagined could be next? Indeed, I hadn't imagined such a thing until I found it.

"I have a low tolerance for injustice and for innocents suffering at the hands of others. No, I don't think that makes me anything more than the average human being, anyone with an ounce of humanity, anyway. But this…? This is the scum of the earth, the lowest we go, in my opinion."

"You're worrying me more than a little."

"I'm sorry. But we are getting to the *why* you asked so long ago. You want to know why we shut it down. Why did *I close* the business and destroy the machines? Yes, you surmised that I fought Peter on this, too. Even after what you're about to hear, I had to fight him on it."

A raised palm 'stop sign' requested a moment as Jessica stood, came beside me, and bent to take a water bottle from the bar beside my chair. I used the pause to finish the contents of the tumbler that had given my hand something to do through those last stories. This one needed some liquid courage to coax it out of my mind to spring from my tongue like an Olympiad hopeful taking his first leap off the high dive.

Necessary.

Terrifying.

Once Jessica settled—in truth, I gave her more time than *she* needed—I began the story, which had until now only fallen on a dead man's ears. Oh, Peter was alive when I told him.

"You must remember… Sorry. We have the most ridiculous expressions, don't we? I'd like you to remember that after my initial motivations to save Ellie failed, I agreed to Peter's relentless insistence on commercializing my invention because I sincerely thought it would help people. I cared not for the money."

"I believe you. Indeed, I do."

Such a sweetheart, this woman—a stranger giving me such unmerited benefit of the doubt. My comments were sincere. I supported and created thousands of travel chambers, fully convinced I was improving people's lives.

"I deeply appreciate that, Jessica. And I believe we did. By far, the vast majority, I'd say, used the machine and its overlaps in beneficial ways. You've seen the flood of overwhelmingly positive customer testimonials."

"Impressive. I wish I could choose a restaurant in New York with such consistent five-star reviews."

"Indeed." Gratitude swelled within me for that brief levity. Perhaps it helped ease me into telling the tale I was passionate to forget. "Ashton Hamilton. He's the reason I shut down the business."

"Sounds like a pompous rich kid who cared more about his almond milk latte than his friends."

That brought a welcome chuckle from me, which induced the same from Jessica. How she could lighten such heavy air in the room.

"He acted nothing like that at all. You've heard the interviews, maybe done some yourself, of the friends and family of monsters after their heinous acts had been exposed. 'He was always such a nice guy,' and all that rubbish."

"Similar to your comments about Adam Solomon… before he killed his former lover. I think there's a lot of truth in it. Evil people, monsters, as you said, get good at hiding under the Doctor Jekyll persona."

"They do indeed. And they got by our screenings."

"Each time, something tipped you off about the client's patterns. Too many trips, too often. What told you you had a Mister Hyde?"

"I wrote a simple program that parsed the logs from every machine in every store and looked for such patterns.

Then, I personally entered the invasion to check them. It became a full-time job. Just as well, I hadn't invented anything new in ages and only worked like a mindless robot producing an occasional new chamber or repairing one flown to me from one of the stores."

"You spent hours a day, every day, watching people's overlaps?"

"I did. And to my delight, even most flagged ones were fine, wholesome recreation for the traveler. Until I got the logs from Ashton Hamilton's trips."

"I shudder to think what you saw that was worse than what you'd already told me."

My bones also quivered, trembling like a banged gong reverberating its crescendo with no signs of quitting. I took a deep breath and the last drop of scotch from my already depleted glass to fortify my tongue for the unpleasant task.

"Ashton was a child sex offender. An abuser."

"Surely any screening would find that. We've had incredible protections on that sort of thing for decades."

"Yes, my dear, for those who'd been caught. Peter used his connections to get the police commissioner to investigate him. We only learned of two boys he'd abused before he started using my machine. He had documented each encounter, and the police found his handwritten paper journal after he'd been arrested."

"And… Marcus, how did he use the chamber?"

"That's where his counsel, a high-paid legal team from Boston, made their defense. They volunteered how he used the machine to fulfill his… unnatural urges. His lawyers claimed he did this to be a good man, to stop himself from ever abusing another child in normal-time."

"That… sounds… an almost credible defense. Don't get me wrong, he should have been castrated and sent to prison for life with no way ever to hurt another child, real or imagined. How did the jury react?"

"After a week-long trial and lots of Peter's money to keep it sequestered, he was convicted of child abuse of those first two boys and sentenced to a lengthy prison term and psychological evaluation."

"Marcus, your invention helped to catch a child abuser and put him away. That was a *good* thing. Why did that make you shut down?"

"It's what he planned to do. Obviously, I couldn't testify in court because of the illegal nature of the evidence I found. I watched all his overlaps in the invasion and saw him not only satisfying his perverse desires but figuring how best to groom his victims and get away with it after."

"Another one testing the waters, perfecting his techniques. A pattern for these people. But again, you got him."

"I'll never know. They only caught him because of his journal. What if he used the methods he practiced in my machine in normal-time? What if he…"

I lost the words. A drowning panic came over me as if my body's fluids had submerged me, yet the tears hadn't reached my eyes.

That soft hand again rested upon my forearm.

"Still, you helped catch a predator. Your machine did that."

"How many others? I'll never know. And remember the difference—my machine versus Transcend. In the overlap, everything is real to the brain. Even if it's a reproduction or speculation of a constructed reality, those other people feel, and experience overlaps as if they were real people."

"Only, they don't come out of the chamber."

"People in the overlaps, the children he abused… For those moments, they *were* real, and suffered from what Ashton Hamilton did to them."

17 | The Unimaginable

STRANGE sensations raged through my veins, hot and full of shame. I used the restroom again. Jessica did as well, having helped herself at liberty to my supply of water bottles. I'd done it, gotten through the worst of it, and gave her the career-defining story she came to get. I didn't yet know what *I got* out of it. Did I get what I wanted by my time with the reporter who faintly favored my wife's appearance?

Self-indulgent fool.

No, it would be good to get the truth out there finally. People will knock me down several pegs on their idol pedestals on which they placed people like me. Perhaps, I thought, this may give them clarity of perception for other prominent people whose characters, whose souls, deserve no such adulation.

One can hope.

Jessica's extended stay in the restroom worried me. I shouldn't have, but I called up the room in my unique version of *trænSend*. When I found the restroom door open, I stood beside her, staring at herself in the mirror. A deep trance fell over her, and I felt her leave the room into her mind.

Water flowing from the tap became a cascade, filling the small space with the thunderous pounding of Niagara Falls. The steam I expected hadn't escaped the basin to cloud the angelic reflection in the mirror—my image not standing beside hers in a 'reality' not as undeniable as an overlap. Vampirical notions plagued me, making me into the monster stalking his prey. No, I was entirely concerned about her emotional state.

Cupped hands lifted splashes of cool water onto Jessica's face, and her wide eyes checked the flattened image, looking back at her, studying her. A deep breath. Another. Had my stories had such an impact? I wished her to know the truth, get the story of her career, and not to horrify her. *What must she think of me now? What does it matter? She'll be gone soon, making me into an anecdote to share with friends and colleagues. 'That time I met Marcus Hollister…'*

Where'd she go? I hadn't noticed her leave.

When I rejoined the study, I sat across from a stranger. Not the Jessica I'd spent the evening with and an entire day in delightful conversation—and some not-so-pleasant topics. A vastly different creature looked back at me as I sunk into my Chesterfield.

"Jessica, are you alright? I'm sorry some of that may have been... hard to hear."

"It was Marcus. Truly. And I'm sorry... I think I'm about to make things worse for you. I hadn't anticipated this, didn't plan what to say or how. I hoped for a much better way to flow into it naturally."

"The book of my life has been opened to you, my dear. I highly doubt you have any chapters to add worse than I've lived. I'm a tired old man, alone, deflated. What could you possibly have to tell me?"

"Please, may we both sip your scotch?"

Like a sucker punch from nowhere, it left me dazed and speechless. My Lagavulin touched her pallet as a vile substance to be spat out on the first—and last—sip she had taken. A morbid dread filled me in contemplation of her words that would follow, words that needed the potent elixir to be summoned out of her.

After a sip and a held-back cough, the interviewer braced herself for something she needed to tell me. She stiffened, shoulders back and chin high. "Marcus, you're correct about me and my research. Not solely for this interview… You've been the key subject of my work, studies, and research for most of my life."

"Really?" No other words came to mind. I couldn't fathom what fascinated her so about me beyond the basics of uncovering the man behind the curtain, responsible for the sensation that had the world beating down my door for their jump into their memories—a meaningless redo of a fraction of their lives, all it was. Pensive, focused eyes upon me shouted for a reply, something more than 'really' after her revelation. Nothing.

"I've imagined this moment, meeting you, since I was a teenager."

"You chose *me* as much as I chose *you*?" My baffled face must have shown my mental state plainly to the keen-eyed reporter.

"I did."

"Wait. You… you didn't make yourself… look like… for me?"

"I did not—just a happy coincidence. I'd been rejected by your office for months trying to get an appointment. Then, out of the blue, you reached out to me when you saw that interview. Saw me."

"And I'm delighted you came. Not only because telling my story is long overdue, I genuinely enjoyed making your acquaintance and spending this time together. Jessica, I think there's something else. You sounded most ominous in the prelude to this conversation. Please, what do you wish to tell me?"

"Okay." Her shoulders wiggled and then set back to their attentive pose. "About those overlaps and the quote-unquote *real* people in them, the ones only in there, not the travelers." Another contemplative pause.

"Yes. Those *real* people are real, in a sense. They have feelings and experience what happened. Again, there is absolutely no effect on them in the real world, in normal-time."

"What if there were?"

My numbed brain rattled the surety of her stated question around like a pinball in an antique game machine, but the flippers missed keeping it in play.

"No. I've been over this, given years of my life to make that so. It's just not possible. Nothing ever changes in the real world, no matter what anyone does in the machine. We simply cannot change the past."

"I'm not talking about the past."

"My dear, I'm afraid you've lost me. That's not easy to do, mind you." My reach for levity crashed and burned in the room, bringing a chill over me, a novel sensation upon my skin. The sinking sun leaving the window's view hadn't altered the room's temperature.

Jessica sat sternly with laser focus. Her need to get through this dripped as sweat over her brow. Flattened palms traveled up and down her thighs, bunching the fabric of Ellie's dress in subtle ripples.

"What if... Have you ever wondered... When you—a traveler, I mean... When the overlap ends, did you ever wonder what happens to the others... in the overlaps?"

"The same as when a Transcend session ends. Everything ends. It's gone like switching off a light. Light doesn't go anywhere. It just... stops shining."

"Yes, but the electricity doesn't. The electrons are still there; just the current is interrupted. What if the traveler is the light, your chamber is the switch, and the overlap is the electricity?"

"Interesting theorizing, though flawed. The electricity analogy isn't quite right. If I'm following your speculation, you suggest that the… universe in the overlap could continue after the traveler has left it?"

"I do."

"Not possible. I've examined all the multiverse theories. How every decision made by every person throughout all human history supposedly spawns a new universe where a different road is traveled than our own…" My head shook in disbelief. "Nonsense. Trillions, no *googillions* of universes, each with copies of Earth filled with billions of people. No. We have but one universe, and it holds but one earth. And… sadly… we only get one go-around."

"Before your invention, that held. Yet, I've learned something you missed. Every trip, every overlap, has left a world continuing without the traveler. And when horrific things were done in an overlap, and the traveler left it, the rest of those people had to pick up the pieces."

"Impossible. I've told you it . . ."

"It can. It did. Survivors of nuclear devastation. Those mass-killings. The family of that woman who was killed in your office repeatedly. Those poor children. Each overlap left them to deal with the aftereffects."

Through the cloud of such nonsensical ideas, I shot out of my chair to my feet. This couldn't be true. I'd proven such, hadn't I? And Jessica Matthews, a pretty face reporting the news on her low subscriber video channel, what could she possibly have known about such complex physics theory? I hadn't realized I started pacing.

When did Jessica rise to her feet? She stood beside me, a hand on each of my arms, with serious eyes full of mystery and suspense piercing right through me.

"Marcus. I know because I'm not a reporter. Not really. I've studied your work, and I figured it out. I learned to cross over from an overlap. I know because I've done it."

Like a blackhole acting upon an asteroid, the inescapable weight of those words pulled me into my chair. *The reporter? No, there's no way she could be telling the truth. Not possible. There is no way to leave our world, normal-time, and enter a universe created by an overlap.* No! *It's just not possible.*

"Wait… Jessica." She knelt beside my chair, hand on my forearm. "Did you say… *from* an overlap?"

18 | The Other Side

MIND-BLOWING revelations ignited the synapses and burned images into my brain. Certainty, perhaps hubris, told me this couldn't happen. It wasn't possible, not even theoretically. My machine, my invention, sent a single traveler to a specific point in their own timeline to relive. Nothing physical was created, and no energy was converted into matter. The physical reality of an overlap was, in reality, a non-reality. I mentally rambled like a madman, hoping words hadn't escaped my lips.

"Yes," she said softly as if to shield the words from invasive ears. We were alone. The only ears her unbelievable words fell upon pushed it away, refuting its implications with decades of study and research.

"Not possible." *Why not? Think... Think... Ah.* "You said... right, you said you came *from* an overlap. In normal-time, you, your double, I guess, here... wouldn't have the same memories because you started your existence from the jump point of the traveler. There is no point in time you could share in the life of Jessica Matthews to jump into her in the real world."

Why did I feel the need to expound on that? She may have played me for a fool or had some hidden agenda. Maybe she was just nuts. Yes, she said she'd been in my machine. Maybe she lost touch with reality and couldn't tell normal-time from an overlap. It happened to a few clients.

"You're missing something. I know it must be a novelty for your brilliant mind. Think of all that could happen in a world created by an overlap."

Without answering, I lifted my head, heavy from the weight my thoughts had added.

"Majel… archive search… life history of Jessica Matthews, New York video blog reporter."

"You call your AIA Majel?"

"Not that New Quantum Corp Artificial Intelligence Assistant rubbish, one of my design—much better." A discrete and well-mannered AI did as instructed and waited for the next command. "List summation, starting with birth records and childhood history."

The perfectly synthesized voice of Majel Barrett-Roddenberry had been the obvious choice, the only choice when I designed the program. "No birth record found for Jessica Matthews. History of New York video blog reporter Jessica Matthews begins the sixth of June of this year in a filing for the video channel *The Real Now, with Jessica Matthews* submitted electronically to the E-Commerce Regulatory Commission of New York City. The next record on file is…"

"Enough."

Needed silence surrounded me. Jessica sat as a statue of herself, her expression as blank as marble, watching me working it out in my head. Logical thought proved elusive, and no sense could be found in the indisputable results. Jessica Matthews, the woman sitting before me, didn't exist.

"You look like you've seen a ghost."

"You'd seen someone then who'd seen a ghost. Sorry, these expressions we thoughtlessly use. I suppose my look would be a good match for such a descriptor. No… you are *not* a ghost, Miss Matthews."

"If not, what other explanation do you have?"

"I may have crossed bounds and shattered even the most intelligent scientific minds with my invention, played with quantum theories, and broken known laws of physics… No, I'm not leaping to the conclusion you are telling the truth, young lady. It isn't all that hard to wipe an identity from the archive."

"That may be true. Humor me, please, for just a moment longer. I need you to understand this, please."

A nod offered agreement when the words hid behind my tongue. Under closed eyes, I stared at the ceiling, head nodding ever so slightly side to side as I thought. While I had no doubt my conclusion would prove true and Jessica's farce would reveal itself, I couldn't guess what she could be playing. I humored her, as requested. I wondered if it could have been some bizarre test.

"Shall I refill your scotch? I know it helps you think."

How did she know it helped me think? True, I'd been sipping it almost constantly since she arrived, at least holding the tumbler. Until now, I would not have described my mental activities as thinking to any great extent. Recalling memories and telling stories required little effort. *She knows me…?*

I think I've got it—from her delusion, anyway. "We've met. In an overlap."

"We have."

Whatever game she played, she was good. Any tricks I employed for teasing, to lead on, to toy with people, this young lady surpassed like a star apprentice outshining the master. We've only just met, so who was the master?

"Realize, of course, I'm playing along for now. I'm not for a second buying into any of this. From your claims, you came from an overlap in which we met. Is… is *this* an overlap? Am I a creation of your trip in my machine?"

"No. We're in normal-time, as I believe you know very well. You've learned that Jessica Matthews didn't exist in this world—the real world, as you call it. Yet, not only now, but you've also seen how familiar we are like we've known each other more than meeting yesterday evening."

"The resemblance to my Ellie. I admit, I've been in a wonderous mental fog since you arrived. I shamelessly lost myself to a fantasy of having a part of her here with me."

"Getting warmer."

"In here? I thought you were chilly with the temperature I keep."

"You've never played hot or cold? You're stumbling in the darkness of your mind's resistance to the truth before you… Despite your best efforts to block it, you're getting warmer." The seriousness departed from her face like a discarded mask for the first time in too many minutes, and warmth filled the smile trailing her words.

"As you said, my mind is fighting to keep it from reaching where *you* want it to go. I have a fiercely powerful mind, as you know, so why don't you give me a little more."

"I'm from a world created by a jump, an overlap, as you call it. When the traveler leaves, the world and its people remain. You and I met in such an overlap, and I continued in my world when you left."

"So, it was *my* overlap. I'm the traveler that created your world."

"You are."

"Okay. You said you studied my work, but I've never shared that with anyone. You could not know anything about my machine beyond what it does. Only I know the *how*."

"True. In normal-time, you'd never tell. You'll take that secret to your grave, and the ability to jump through time will die with you. Your legacy."

"Now you're in cahoots with my warring brain, supporting my position. You couldn't have used my technology and cannot be from an overlap. It's impossible, even tugging the most outer fringes of any fringe science."

"Time travel was impossible before you invented it. Heck, electricity was impossible. Flight."

"Are you putting yourself up there with Edison, Tesla, the Wright brothers, *me?*"

"While good inventors borrow, what do great inventors do?"

"Steal. Again, I've never shared the knowledge of my invention, not even in an overlap."

"Not even... *once?*"

Once?

Oh... It can't be. Jessica *cannot be. No, this simply isn't possible.*

Yet... Once.

19 | The One Time

ONCE. I did, as Jessica said, discuss my work in one overlap, and only that one time. That one time, in the new memories being made, a place I wished never to leave. It was the only time I tried to build my machine in an overlap. I built it by pushing the bounds yet further, tearing at the fringes of science.

You see, I hypothesized that the *reality* of the world in the overlap would make it possible. The version of me in the overlap could use the machine to return to a point in the same trip—that ageless 'folded paper' concept to travel through time and space. Only we never got folding space to travel from one point to another to work. Maybe if *I'd* worked on that...

My machine did fold time over itself, allowing the traveler to step back into a point in their timeline. 'Jumping' into themselves at a moment they remembered well, the more vivid their memory, the greater the chance to get a lock for their jump. It's why emotionally charged moments worked best, as they engraved more vivid and lasting memories.

I could do it. Get a working chamber in the overlap, test it, and then use it to go back into the same overlap a few weeks before I'd have to leave it. I'd extend my time in that reality by another fifteen years, in an overlap within an overlap. I could build it again and get another fifteen years.

I'd grow old with Ellie.

It became an obsession; my life's work condensed to a few years. You see, I'd invented the thing already. I merely needed time and money to gather the tools and materials, make the parts, and assemble them. Oh, and a means to draw massive amounts of electricity to power the thing. It's a good thing I already had become well-off before Ellie's… Every trip started with me being rich, and in some, I used my foreknowledge of events to add to that wealth. After all, I wasn't altering normal-time, so I figured, what the heck.

That was it! It was the one time I shared the technology behind the machine with someone. That was the only time I ever told anyone in an overlap about it.

"Once. Yes, I did."

"I know." On her knees, Jessica pivoted to face me and took my other arm with her hand. A hopeful glint danced over her eyes as the last of the twilight's rays hit them. "I was there."

No. It couldn't be. It simply wasn't possible. How could Jessica have known any of this? A guess. Anyone could have guessed I might try to create my machine in an overlap. Anyone could claim they were there. Only one person could know. No. People… the world created in the overlap wasn't real physically. It is a blip, no more than watching old-movie-created versions of actors long dead. Nothing remained after an overlap. And even if I shared the technology of my machine, it never came close to being able to traverse a multidimensional vortex into another universe—one that didn't exist because there was and ever would be only one.

"No. This is… It can't be, I tell you. I don't know what wicked game you're playing here, toying with my emotions as you are, but this needs to end. *Now*."

Harsh words blanked Jessica's face. I didn't mean to do it; even as she played her malevolent tricks to an end, I still failed to extrapolate. Something made me care for this woman, and a hollow formed in my heart for hurting her.

"Emotions are high for both of us. Why do you think that is? If I was making this up and throwing guesses at you, how did I hit such a chord on your heartstrings." Jessica looked deeply into my eyes as if she could see my soul behind the glossy orbs. "Why is your mind fixated on one possible conclusion? That *one time* you talked about… and *built* your machine in an overlap."

"The only possible conclusion is you are a master storyteller, and somehow, you or someone you hired got into my private files. Is that why you agreed to stay the night? You hacked my system while I slept?"

The cunning woman stood, stepped to the window, and gazed at the sunset all but gone, leaving a haze of purple and red scattered over the last of the retreating daytime sky's blue. I threw nonsensical allegations at her to buy my mind much-needed processing time. Did she say I built the machine? She knew I built one in that overlap. No. A guess. She reached, reading me and feeding me bologna like a hungry child whose taste hadn't developed enough to loathe the disgusting loaf of junk meat scraps.

She spoke from her back. "You know your system is impenetrable. Only you are clever enough to hack a system of your own design. And we both know you don't have any such data to find. No records of your overlaps, all deleted, as you said earlier."

Of course, she was correct. I grasped at the only straws I could use to pull myself from the mire her words sunk me into. The hold of that mental bog squeezed me so tight I couldn't breathe. When I gulped the last of the tumbler's scotch in place of the desperately needed air, it poured into my lungs and launched me into a coughing fit.

Firm thuds landed on my shoulder blade from Jessica's pounding palm. I raised my hand to signal I'd be fine if she would please just stop banging my back. My mind flashed to a scene so vivid I could have been in the fluid chamber—a memory from a trip, from an overlap. *It can't be. It can't.*

Could it be?

Within a few seconds, my lungs settled, and racing thoughts slammed across my mind in a headache of chaos no pill could persuade away. If it were possible, if the people created by the overlap continued, what did that make of the traveler? How many versions of Ellie had I abandoned?

"If I were to play along… If people continued living when the traveler left the overlap… what happened to them, to the traveler? Did they simply disappear?"

"No. You know your science better than anyone. You once described it like a symbiotic possession, the traveler inhabiting the mind of themselves in the overlap." Correct.

Her research skills continued to shine. "When the traveler left, the person, them, stayed. Memories and all."

"With the traveler returning to normal-time with the memories, none the wiser, the others continued living in some alternate universe they created."

"Exactly."

"And you figured this out yourself?"

"I did. Based on your work, your machine… You helped."

Jessica took her seat with eyes focused on me in a way they hadn't up to then. They were filled with both sorrow and hope. Graciously, she gave me her silence when I needed to say what I couldn't believe came across my lips.

"*Sabrina?*"

20 | The Crossover

WITH a sheepish smile, she lowered her head to say, "Dad."

Stone and immovable. My bones fused, and the muscles clinging to them by the tendons stiffened as dried cement. No words. No action. Nothing. The cold chill of death's approach penetrated my internal organs as if life itself were finally done with my tired flesh.

Stubbornly, my mind fought the realization it had just made, refuting it with logic and science. This couldn't be possible. The family I raised on that trip, the happiest memories of my life, only existed in the overlap. The only *real* person is the one that emerges from the chamber. That has been my reality, my life, my failure.

New eyes, youthful and bright, gazed upon me, full of wonder. Jessica had revealed her massive news, a revelation to blow my mind and shock my body. *What must she be thinking? She cannot be my Sabrina. This simply isn't possible. My machine could never do what she claims.*

The formerly charismatic and full-of-life persona of Jessica Matthews withered into a shy girl sent to the sofa for a time-out. Why did I see her that way? No, she couldn't be Sabrina. The silence of the room could have been a hammer inside my head, the throbbing pressure reaching critical and about to explode.

The uncanny resemblance. Twelve. When I left that overlap, my baby girl was twelve years old. How often my mind aged her, shaped an image into the woman she would have become if only she existed in normal-time. Did Jessica Matthews remind me of Ellie or the mental construct of a Sabrina who had grown to womanhood?

Not a living soul knew the true nature of my mourning, the loss of my Ellie in normal-time, compounded by leaving her all those times, grieving her after each trip in the machine. Peter never learned of the family we began in that overlap. That one time. How could Jessica Matthews have known?

"How?" I hadn't planned to say that. I didn't believe her, wouldn't admit it to myself. 'It's not possible' rang over every thought. Yet, the familiarity, the face, the mannerisms, the gentle care she'd shown me. The parts of the brain allowing the emotional decay of my sorry existence and its new growth needed to ask but one simple question. How?

After clearing her throat, Jessica raised her head to lock eyes with me. "You remember—of course, you do—working with me on your machine. At first—I think I was about seven—you showed me some drawings and schematics of the machine. You filled my sponge brain with stories of how it worked and what it would accomplish long before I knew you were in an overlap."

Only one person could have known that—a person who didn't exist in normal-time.

"You swore me to secrecy, said I couldn't even tell Mom or George."

Her little brother. No, Sabrina's little brother. Could she have used experimental mind-mapping on me while I slept? I'd read the theses and studied the underlying premise. It seemed years from viability. My mind found its answer, and it had to be. The nose and chin are not the same as Ellie's. She always said Sabrina luckily got those from me.

"I told George, though, sorry. But only when I knew my modification had worked and that I would come here. He thought it was one of my playful gags. I can imagine his face now."

"How old are you, *Jessica*?"

Her face scrunched at the call of her name. "Thirty-four. George turned twenty-nine last month."

"In just twenty-two years, you claim to have learned to use my machine to traverse universes? In more than five decades, I've never managed that."

"No. But have you ever tried or even thought of doing it?"

Clever. Jessica knew how to bait me and twist logic in her favor. Traces of that aspect of my personality had begun to show in Sabrina. While it drove Ellie crazy, it always made her smile. No. Jessica Matthews could not be my daughter.

"I'll take the pensive silence as a 'no.' The only motivation you tried, the only one you desperately wanted to work, was to travel back, to jump into a point in time within the same overlap."

"To extend it as long as possible, yes. To stay with Ellie, you—no, *my daughter*—and son."

"It didn't work. I remember how hard you tried. When I was eleven, you explained the theory to me, told me you had traveled, and we were in your overlap. Some of our happiest times were working on the machine together."

A device. She must have brought a brain scanner here. Where could it be hiding? She entered yesterday with only a tablet, a leather-bound writing pad, and a pencil. No, she had a handbag.

"Where is it?"

"Where is what?"

"Your handbag. The device you used to scan me."

"I don't know what you're talking about. Dad, I just—"

"No. Don't 'Dad' me. There is no way you can be who you claim, and I'll get to the truth of who you are and what you might possibly hope to gain from this charade. Majel… Locate Miss Matthews' bag. Tell me where it is."

The synthesized voice replied, "Miss Matthew's bag is in the guest suite beside the bed, on the left side."

I rose and entered the guestroom as the doors parted.

"Oh, that's a bit creepy that your AIA can see into the guestroom. But look through my bag. I've got nothing to hide. And you'll not find anything to combat what I think you already know and that you merely need to accept."

As I reached for the bag, I asked Majel to scan the room for any personal items of Miss Matthews and anything not there before her arrival. The results led me into the wardrobe to find her skirt and blouse from the previous evening neatly folded over the dressing room chair and her bra and underwear on the floor where she had tossed them before her shower.

Stupidity reared its ugly head even in the brightest of minds. It didn't take much in my personal life to surface my inner moron. Rather than examine her things in isolation, I carried them back to the study and sat before her.

"Checking my underwear for a brain scan device, *really?*"

I ignored the sarcastic remark and checked the stitching and edging of the garments, then emptied the contents of her handbag. Small and dainty, it held few items. Car keys, a mobile hand device, a comb, and a small mirror. Nothing large enough to hide a scanner. I pulled open a drawer in the cherrywood desk beside my chair and retrieved a small hammer.

Blankly, she watched as I smashed her tablet, key fob, phone, and mirror, then tore apart her bag. "Majel… Full body scan of Jessica Mathews. Identify any technology or inorganic items on or in her person."

"In? Really?"

The Majel AIA replied, "Nothing detected."

"I understand your hesitance and need to violate my privacy and check my things. Destroy my stuff. I can't imagine what a shock this must be for you. I've imagined this day, prepared for it, and mentally rehearsed it for years. You've had it dumped on you from out of nowhere. Take your time."

"I... I don't understand how anyone could know what you know. There's no way... I - " I hung my head under the shame of manhandling the young woman's undergarments, rifling through her purse, and smashing her things. "There's... no way."

"There's one." Her warm hand rested upon my forearm, Jessica leaning forward with a longing regard over her face. "*Dad...* there's one way I could know these things. Just the one, and you know it. Let yourself accept it, please, for me. See me as your daughter, as Sabrina. I'm here, Dad, after all these years. I crossed over, and I'm as real as you."

21 | The Acceptance

AGAINST my better judgment, I decided to stop the two sides fighting for dominance in my brain. There must have been other explanations for all of this, some way to make it all make sense. None found their way to my mind, so I pushed the justified skepticism aside for the moment to follow this through to see where it would take me.

"Okay, Jessica, I need to understand some things. Ellie and I did indeed have a daughter named Sabrina in that overlap. Then a boy we called George, after El—"

"For her father, my grandpa George."

"He was so happy to have a grandson namesake."

"He died before my brother was born, just after my fourth birthday, and before Mom got pregnant."

Okay, she could have guessed the entrapment… but the detail she knows. *How?* That mental feud tried to flare up again, so I quenched its fire with a healthy spray of tentative acceptance. Still, I had to probe, confirm, and know—convinced I'd find the flaw, expose her deceit.

Every memory I began, Jessica finished with absolute accuracy. Sabrina's first time riding a bike without training wheels, George's complicated birth, Ellie's extended hospital stay, and our trip to Disneyland. We laughed when she recounted the time we got rained on and George's cotton candy tangled in Ellie's hair. The rain made quick work of melting it away. I'd never seen my beloved partner laugh so intensely.

"We were such a happy family."

I said, 'We.' In a dream, I once floated in the heavens and rested upon a cloud, sinking into the soft cotton-like mist. This brought the same sensation. Subconsciously, I lapsed into the acceptance of the proposed reality. Not yet; this needed more vetting. Logic denied what the heart yearned to have, and, in my experience, following my heart never ended well.

"We did. I have such good memories of my childhood. You were a great dad, and Mom was the best."

"Wait, why the past tense? You said Mom *was* the best. Where is she now, and me—I mean your father?"

"No, Mom's fine. She's a grandma now. Not me—George has a little boy…" Jessica's lips bent into a gentle smile. "Marcus."

Too much. All of this. Could my machine have done this? Could my family have lived on in a world created by my overlap, by my invention?

"You're avoiding mention of your father in your present day. What happened to him after I left?" I did it again, speaking as if everything she told me could be true.

"You…" Jessica swallowed her word with a closed-eyed gulp. "He, my father… over there. He died not long after. We had a few more years together."

"I'm sorry. And Ellie? How did she cope?"

"She's a strong woman, you know that. I assume every overlap version of her has her strength. She was great with George, helping him through losing his dad at such an early age. She… well… Mom remarried three years after."

"Good. That's good for her. She… was she happy?"

"Yes. Mom never stopped loving you, she assured George and me often, for years. She carried on. Sadly, she's widowed again. Happened last year."

"And you? What about you? You, too, were young when your father died. How did you handle it?"

"You remember what you always said whenever I tinkered with an appliance or tore down and rebuilt some electronic device?"

"You're just like me."

"I was. I am. And like you, I lost myself in my work."

"You were, what, about fifteen?"

"You taught me all you knew about your machine, the science behind it, and how it worked. I helped you build it. I was there when it almost killed you trying to send you back to a moment in the overlap you were already in."

"School? Boyfriends? Tell me you had a life. Not like me."

"I did. Mom made sure of it. Of course, she didn't know what my *hobby*, she called it, really was, but knew I was carrying on something you and I had done, so she encouraged it, in moderation."

"She has no idea you're here."

"No. Mom knows nothing about the machine, the overlaps, or that she is one of your redo lives. Sorry, I didn't mean that to sound crass. I mean, I have a life I wouldn't have had if you never traveled. What you experienced as a fifteen-year overlap gave me life and made my world."

"You were the only one who ever knew? Until you told George recently."

"Yes. No one knew the details of the obsession that consumed me all those years. You and I worked on what you called 'our special project', and we never told Mom, George, or anyone what it was. You told me about the time limit in the overlap and why you wanted to travel back within ours to extend your time with us."

"Everything I tried… and I tried everything I could think of, believe me. Nothing worked. It's simply impossible to travel into an overlap within an overlap."

"You never stopped trying. We worked on it right up until you had to go. You taught me everything you knew. And when you left you… um, *he,* I guess, kept teaching me quantum theories and fringe sciences, and I soaked it up like a sponge."

"He had all of the memories of my life in normal-time, losing Ellie, all I did here, and knew he was the product of the overlap?"

"He knew he was you, yes. And he knew he had got to live a life with Mom he, you, had lost. He was always so grateful, so cheerful. And he made Mom happy every single day."

"Then he died. How?"

"You remember how you got the uranium? You made some enemies. Even after you paid them more than you promised, they… demanded more. They came to make a point: they were going to kill Mom and threaten George and me to motivate you to build them a weapon. You sacrificed yourself for us."

Jessica made no effort to hide her eyes glazed over from the relived memory, and she blinked rapidly. She'd lost so much and somehow maintained such gratitude and zest for life—something I failed to do as I let my losses consume me and bury me in a lonely hermitage.

Ah, one more test to be sure I hadn't allowed myself to be duped by the desperation for this alleged truth, prematurely buying into her story because I *wanted* her to be my little girl. You see, the logical part of my brain persisted in its fight against the enormity of the emotional pull, nudging it along the clifftop to plunge it over the edge in victory.

"In my workshop, I used to sing along to a classic Bee Gees song called More Than a Woman…"

She sang in falsetto from a face radiating sunlight, "Four-legged woman. Four-legged woman. Two knees."

We both laughed at the callback. My sweet girl's young ears had misheard the lyrics, and she had sung those ridiculous words in a full and hearty bellow that filled the workshop with unbounded joy.

Again, she took my hand. "I remember how it made you laugh back then. It's about like now, but less wheezy. We sang it that way from then on... Did it ever dawn on you that I sang it that way on purpose to make you laugh?"

"You knew the words?"

"Of course, Dad. I was, like, eleven."

"Why, Sabrina...? Why come here, then? You had some time, limited, yes, but you spent time with your actual father, memories made together without me for a couple of years. That man... he, he's your dad."

"So are you." The sniffles came, and I handed her my handkerchief. "You... you called me Sabrina."

22 | The Kitchen

ALL battles, from spousal disagreements to the unthinkable world wars, eventually ended. My mind had given in to the domination of emotion and accepted the unbelievable as true. My daughter had taken my knowledge and training and exceeded my wildest expectations for what my invention could do. Sabrina had crossed over from her world, another universe with its genesis via my machine, to see me.

Payment demanded for the effort amounted to more than twenty years of her life.

Why? What pulled her here when she had her father? It was an abbreviated time, but time well spent with memories built, new ones created without me. Those few years with him after I left, experiences I never had and could never relive, shared with her real dad. I was nothing more than the man who played house with a pretend family I thought to have vanished when I woke up in the tank.

Burning in my intestines, a deep desire to know everything overcame me. How did Sabrina adapt my machine, my science, to create the crossover device? What was I like after I left? Wow, the wobbliness of the logic confused even me sometimes. Who was this woman my daughter had become?

Could I cross back with her?

We sat silhouetted in the darkness the sun left behind as it closed the day to announce the evening had arrived. At almost eight, my chef had the day off. Rivaling the insatiable thirst for answers, my belly growled in protest of missing my usual seven o'clock dinner time. Hours flew in Jessica's company and disappeared even quicker in Sabrina's.

"Dad, do you have what we need for a pesto?"

Hours of tension fled my muscles as we smiled at each other at the thought of what only I called 'my famous pesto.'

"Always. With basil fresh from the garden. I'll go pick it if you start on the potatoes."

We each stood to handle our assigned tasks when Sabrina faced me and looked me almost even in the eye, nearly as tall as me. I looked upon the face of my darling twelve-year-old daughter when I said goodbye to her the last time I saw her, more than twenty years ago.

"Dad? Before we… Can I…?"

Before her words could finish, I grabbed her and pulled her in tight into an inner warmth two decades told me I'd never feel again. We let time stop to give the two of us the moment, reunited in unimagined bliss I hadn't dared dream of ever experiencing again. I held my Sabrina once more.

The heart-shaped face nestled into my bosom, and her arms stretched around me to clasp each other around my back. A grunt came with pressure as she squeezed with all her might as she always did as a child. Of course, her arms had greater strength now, and my bones had aged to where almost everything hurt. It was such a lovely embrace; we wished it never to end.

When I entered the kitchen, freshly picked basil in hand, Sabrina already had a few small yellow potatoes peeled and boiling. *I must be getting slow in my old age.*

"I'll blanch the green beans if you'll get the pesto sauce going."

"As you wish, my dear girl." I couldn't stop myself.

Waterfalls of tears fell from my eyes, and I gasped to inhale enough air to burst my lungs. The memory of the last time we made pesto together, the four of us, two days before I left, overpowered every part of me, physically, mentally, and emotionally. I found myself again in Sabrina's firm embrace, her face an equal mess of tears as she tried to inhale the mucus running over her upper lip.

Composed, we finally continued preparing the meal over memories of those times. We all shared the kitchen duties back home, back in that overlap. We had such wonderful memories of happy times. I wondered if I'd have been as good a dad, just as vested in my family if Ellie and I had children in normal-time. Work always got in the way.

"Dear, did you salt the water?"

"Yeah, *Dad*. I always remembered. And you always asked."

I dropped two handfuls of trofie pasta into the water. "I did, didn't I? Every time."

"It's cute." That came with a peck on the nose. I used to have to bend down when she wanted to do that.

A calming surrealness saturated me beyond any *trænSɛnd* experience—not even my illegal version or machine overlaps. We were grounded in the reality of normal-time, yet floating through the moment as in a dream.

Screams from the blender cut through the room. I gestured to Sabrina to strain the pasta—the fresh stuff only needed a few minutes. She dumped it into a serving bowl with the cut potatoes and string beans. Then I poured on the pesto sauce liberally, unleashing a torrent of aroma as the raw basil paste grabbed onto the piping-hot pasta and flowed like lava around the mound of noodles. We quickly took our seats to dig in and satisfy our watering mouths. No longer positioned on opposite ends of the oval table, Sabrina sat directly beside me, 'her chair' next to Dad as she always claimed in childhood.

"Proper Pesto Genevese," I declared as a victory.

"Been too long. We tried, but no one makes it as good as yours."

The enjoyment derived from conversation far exceeded that from the pesto, though it did come amazingly good. Fresh-picked basil elevated it every time. Over the sensational meal, I learned all about Sabrina's life in the years I'd missed. Ellie had indeed kept her balanced—a master skill employed on me throughout our relationship, at least in normal-time. I cared not for work pursuits in my overlaps with her.

"What you said, as Jessica, about the love that left you?" I was unsure if everything she said in her reporter persona reflected her real life. "Even as Jessica Matthews, I couldn't imagine anyone idiotic enough to leave you. As Sabrina, it's even more unfathomable."

"Well." She fully swallowed her bite of pasta. "That was a stretch, as Jessica, not to give myself away. By the man I loved, who had to leave me to return to his work… I meant *you*."

Devastating guilt flooded into me for the first time. No, it had been there since I accepted my darling's impossible visit. Its power fought my mind not to accept the truth of her identity because then I'd have to accept its remorse.

"You said Mom kept you balanced. You had a life beyond your obsession to build the machine and come here. Were there boys and men? Or…?"

"There were boys and men, Dad. I mean, boys when I was younger, then men as an adult. Never anyone serious. Not for my obsessions, just, none of them *saw me…*, you know? No one could see the outer me, the inner me—my personality, likes, dislikes, sense of humor, the real me—and appreciate my ever-active mind."

"One of the many plagues of genius." She smirked at me for that. "No, it's not hubris. As a child, I immediately saw the brain you had, like mine, with even more potential. Mom saw it, too, and knew what it looked like from me. It takes a special person to see past it, to see you."

"Like Mom."

"Like your mom. I think it's one of the reasons I hid myself, as you said. Well, as Jessica said. I knew no one else would get me as she did. Until Jessica Matthews, that is. That's what blew me away, way beyond the physical like-ness. I had no idea why at the time, but it was so natural, so organic. It took me back to Ellie, in normal-time, and swept me off my feet."

"Wait, Dad… Were you… *attracted* to Jessica?"

"Yes. I mean, no, not like that. Look, I'm an old man and have loved one woman all my years. I couldn't under-stand what I felt for Jessica until now. Knowing who you are, now it makes sense. Jessica's pull on me was you, the bond between father and daughter."

"And in a stranger, you couldn't quantify that."

"Exactly. And… I'm not sure I can now. This is still so mind-blowing, being here with you. You are here from an alternate universe. That you even exist as a real person shatters my understanding of science, of reality."

"Yet - here I am."

"Here you are."

23 | The Old Man

WHAT might my darling Breanie have expected to find here? A decade and a half, no, two decades had passed for her since seeing her dad, seeing me. Yet I'm far beyond those years in appearance and well below the health a man of her father's age should possess.

Were all those years of her life wasted for this moment, a few measly hours with her father? That tired expression of calling a dad "the old man" now rang true for her. Truer than she must have thought before seeing me, seeing what I've become—this dilapidated body, worn and used and ready for permanent retirement—my time approached, relentless and unavoidable. What a disappointment I must have been for her.

She called me a recluse, thought me an isolationist, a hermit. In other words, my baby girl thought her "old man" to be a sad, pathetic, lonely, wasted life. No, she wasn't wrong in that. *Jessica*. Did Sabrina feel that way about me? Jessica had said those things, implying I had hidden myself from the world. No, not implied; she used those exact words. Where did the divide split Sabrina from Jessica? Which words and thoughts sprang from the false persona, and which originated deep in my daughter's heart?

Mind you, I could relate. While most of my overlaps brought me wonderful moments, precious new memories, and fully rich and wonderful experiences with youth and vitality to share with my dear Ellie, some fell far short of that. We'd been attacked, survived horrific accidents, and even died. Yet, for me, I had a redo button. I could hop back into the machine and start over.

Sabrina had but one shot at this.

Not only would her physical body not be able to survive another lengthy bath in the chamber fluid, but I'd calculated a high probability of fatality on a second traversal of the void. No doubt, she had reached the same conclusion. Besides, all she could hope to find on another voyage would be an older, more decrepit version of me. And, while I'd keep this from her, she'd likely find me dead and buried on a future trip, even if in the not-too-distant future. You see, I'd grown old and hadn't taken the best care of myself.

One more trip? The pull of a final overlap, to live again as a younger version of myself with health, energy, and a loving wife… I never fully got over my habit of stretching the truth. Ellie always told me that saying it that way didn't make it any less wrong. Lying was lying. So, I'd be lying to say I didn't want to go back in for one last lifetime with my love. To extend my last weeks of life to fifteen years and go out with a bang rather than a whimper.

No. I had resolved not to. Yet I did. To have one last overlap, a short one, into memory rather than a new moment. I had to do it. I needed to confirm my failing mental faculties hadn't skewed my memories of my beautiful Ellie. This Jessica Matthews—so young but so much like her in form, voice, tone, and cadence. I had to go back to see Ellie with younger eyes. I had to confirm the resemblance I found in Jessica's symmetrical face didn't come from desperation and grief alone.

My selfishness started one more world.

Another universe spawned from hubris and greed.

Maybe, as Sabrina related, I gave another Ellie and Marcus a new and wonderful life. Looking at things through her lens softened the guilt—a guilt I'd only known for a day yet felt the weight of its devastation as crushing as the one I carried for failing Ellie all those years ago. I didn't save her in normal-time and failed each time I tried in an overlap, unable to reunite with her in our world. Unlike other failures, no successes were born from that, only decades of mournful regret.

Jessica, no, Sabrina returned from the restroom to break me out of my spiraling torment, lifting me from the pit of despair I so willingly had allowed myself to sink into. As I so often did.

"You okay, Dad?"

"Fine, darling. No. You're here. I'm fantastic."

"Me too. I'm so glad we have this time together. I looked forward to it for so many years. And now…" Her shoulders withdrew, and she glowed in a warm smile. "I'm here."

I pulled her in for a hug, basking in its warmth and the love I missed but never knew how deeply. A soft touch of a finger lay upon my face. A gentle motion removed a single tear from my cheek.

"I know," Sabrina whispered.

"No, my dear. Not this. I've shed tears for losing you, George, and your mom… repeatedly for losing countless versions of Ellie. Most of the mourning I've done has been for your overlap; I mean your world, the life I had with you and your brother with your mom at my side. The tear you banished came from a vastly different source."

"What do you mean?"

"Look at me. You, my little girl, all grown up. Your father should still be a vibrant, healthy man. Older, sure, but by a small margin over your memories of me and your dad after me."

"You're my dad."

"I know, that's not what I mean. It's… you must not have expected to find such an aged man. I'm much older than your dad should be."

"You *are* my dad. And I knew you'd be older than you normally would have been from my world. You told me you were much older when you entered the machine and entered my universe, created it."

"I did?"

"Yep."

"The memory's not what it once was, my dear. Still, this tired old body, these weary bones, my sagging flesh, I'd have kept myself in better health had I known I would even have a minute with you…."

Sabrina leaned over to kiss my forehead gently and pulled on my arm to raise me from the dinner table.

"I love you, Daddy."

"Love you too, Baby Girl."

Wide eyes gazed upon me with the wonder of a child. Again, I saw only my little girl looking up at me as we worked together on my futile efforts to build my machine in her overlap. Her amazement at the stories of my life in normal-time and the overlaps I'd visited always lit her face and sparked a barrage of probing questions. Perhaps that spawned the *interviewer* in Jessica.

"Come, *Old Man*, let's go sit."

24 | The Scotch

RETIRED once more to the study, I headed for my Chesterfield when a firm grip on my arm froze me mid-step.

"Something wrong, dear?"

"You in the chair, me on the sofa… That was Jessica Matthews interviewing Marcus Hollister. Me and my dad sit beside each other on the sofa."

I replied with a dimple-digging smile, and we sat beside each other. Sabrina's hand snaked its way between my arm and torso, and she wrapped her arm around mine, melting me like ice cream left on the porch in the summertime.

"See, isn't this better." Another warm smile came with wide eyes that looked up at me from under her raised brow. Ellie used to look up at me that way. *She is so much like her mother, yet she thinks like me.*

"You always have the best ideas, Breanie."

A single tear trickled out from her eye, and she let gravity pull it down beside my darling girl's nose to find her perfect chin. "I haven't heard that name in ages. You're the only one who ever called me that."

"I know. It was my thing. I never knew if you liked or tolerated it to humor me."

"I love it. It's just between us. I've missed you so much, Daddy."

When Sabrina leaned her head on my shoulder, I crowned it with my lips in a gentle kiss upon her scalp. "Me too, Breanie, so much it hurt every day. My loneliness, my grief, that everyone attributes to Ellie's death… Of course, that's a huge part of it." I rested my head upon hers. "But I mourn the loss of every Ellie from every overlap. And even more, I lost my family. My beautiful little girl and that rambunctious ball of energy we called George."

"I lost you twice."

"I'm so sorry, sweetheart. If only I'd known what I was leaving in my wake, all those trips, all those worlds, all those Ellies I left behind. And to abandon you, my family. I'm just so… so sorry."

"If you'd have known about the people going on after you left, you'd not have done it or stopped when you figured it out?"

"Of course. I never meant to play Brahma, creator of worlds. And to start a life and abandon it, abandon her over and over like that. Of course, I'd not have done it at all. Or I would have destroyed all those chambers as soon as I learned this."

"Then I'm glad you didn't know. You'd have missed out on the experience of raising a family, and I'd… well, I'd never have existed, would I?"

"My dear girl, I'm so grateful for that, truly. My years in that overlap, with your mom and you, were my life's best moments—two weeks in the tank but fifteen years of blissful life. No, I don't regret that. But there's a limit, a point where science goes too far."

"Creating thousands of new worlds, your multiverse, you think you crossed that line?"

"Of course. Not only did I play God and created worlds. Think of the consequences of those people continuing after the overlaps ended: the murder victims' families, those children. And I abandoned my family. I left you."

"No. You gave me life, and I love my life, love being alive. I'd not have that otherwise. And leaving me…? You didn't abandon me, us. When you left, *this* you, back to your normal-time, my dad stayed with me. He was you in every respect. You and I shared my first twelve years, and I kept my dad a few more after that." Her arm pulled tighter against mine. "And now I have you."

"I still can't believe it. I see you, smell you, feel you. It's just too surreal, yet more real than an overlap, more real even than my life has been in normal-time."

"You're not having your after-dinner scotch?"

"I've got no craving for it. I've had at least one every afternoon and evening for as long as I can remember, yet I've lost the taste for it now."

"I remember you loving your occasional scotch, but when I came here… I didn't remember you drinking so much of it. I figured it was because of my childhood memories, you know? Children see the world differently, I think."

"They do. It's one of the amazements of parenthood to experience the world anew through your child's eyes. Yours were always full of such wonder. They still are."

"And your drinking? The isolation? I had no idea what to expect when I got here. I couldn't know if you were even alive in your world when I left home. So, I'm not judging or proposing to know how hard your life here has been."

"That leads to a *but…* Go on."

"I arrived a few months ago and started researching you and phoning and sending correspondence to your office daily. My research gave me some troubling facts but didn't tell me who you were. Your office never responded."

"My office is an answering service that is under strict orders not to relay a message to me unless it meets a very stringent set of variables, to reply to no inquiry, and never to accept contact from reporters."

"I see. Then you finally reached out to me because I looked like Mom."

"Yes. I fibbed a bit earlier. Don't get me wrong, you did an amazing job on that interview video, especially as a clever guise, but your likeness to your mother is what got you an invitation to my home."

"As I hoped. I picked that CEO—pestered him relentlessly until he said yes—knowing you'd watch. Then, when you saw me, you insisted I spend the night after arranging for me to be here on the night of a predicted storm. It was something watching you finagle the evening to keep me here late enough that I'd have no choice but to accept the offer."

"Was I that transparent?" We both laughed the answer out. "A foolish old man's indulgence. My darling, I noticed some of what you learned about me may have disappointed you. I told you, as Jessica, a few times that I merited no respect or awe. I'm afraid I'm just a flawed man, more so than most."

"You're a great man, accomplished remarkable things. But you're an even greater dad, and husband, and person. Anyone who knows your story can sympathize and understand your reclusive nature."

"But you didn't expect a drunk."

"You're not even that. You mostly nursed those drinks of scotch, that horridly smokey stuff you drink. You never lost lucidity or sobriety. However, I think it did become a crutch for you… a coping mechanism. And I'm glad you've not felt the need for another drink after dinner."

"With you here, even for these few moments, I could put the tumbler down and never need another drink for the rest of my days."

"I believe you. And, while it was extremely hard to find… I know, Dad. I know about the liver disease and your heart problems."

25 | The Inevitability

ALWAYS drinking, yet never a drunk. Some might call it alcoholism. Of course, Sabrina was correct again. I never sought counseling and scoffed at the advice so many offered—unsolicited, mind you—to 'talk to someone.' I did the opposite for most of the days I spent without Ellie. Days that piled up to form decades.

Other than in the chamber, those magnificent escapes in my machine, in an overlap, my only solace came from a bottle. Extremely expensive bottles—I only bought the good stuff. Lagavulin 32 wasn't even on the market, and only people with connections and lots of money ever enjoyed its smooth flavor.

Overindulgence, I guess, would be another way to describe it. Dependency. I hadn't thought about it until Sabrina expressed her concerns. I mentioned the stupidity that visits my otherwise magnificently reliable brain all too often. I'd convinced myself that my health issues, clearly explained by the highest-paid and most renowned doctors on the planet as alcohol-related, were simply the effects of old age, certainly amplified by the physical strain placed upon my body for living so many extra years in the machine.

I convinced myself the flesh had worn out its usefulness.

Only I hadn't.

Fooling oneself isn't possible, so I buried it under excuses.

I hardly ever drank in the overlaps. Foolish, I know, as I could have indulged as much as I wished with no impact on my liver or heart in normal-time—one of the many things I got totally backward in my mess of a life. In normal-time, in what I accepted as my real life, my liquid escapism ruined my health. Now, the inevitable conclusion of my self-destruction fast approached.

It's excellent scotch.

We sat silently, enjoying a closeness transcending the physical intimacy we shared on the sofa. How long Sabrina would stay, what would happen next—questions too frightful to ask, answers I couldn't hear, not yet. They'd take me from this moment, and I couldn't allow that.

"How long, Dad?"

"For what, my sweet girl?"

"Your diagnosis… How long do you have?"

"Let's not talk of such things, dear. I want to absorb every morsel of joy from this moment."

"I know. Me too. But…"

"You must return to your world."

"Of course. I'm in a tank, in the fluid. But I've been *here* for almost four months in a crossover. Time doesn't dilate as it does in an overlap. I'm heavily medicated and have all sorts of unmentionable tubes and devices in me. I've been in the tank about as long as I've been here. At least that's what the theory shows."

"Impressive. My medical team never got my body to endure more than two weeks in the tank. Do you know how much time we have?"

"This is my first and only trip, so I'm working off speculation."

"You're skillfully avoiding telling me this is almost over. You think you'll be pulled back across soon."

Silence. Sabrina's withdrawn countenance said she didn't want to face the inevitable either. She had explained to me how, unlike jumping into an overlap, she could only traverse to the exact same point in time as in the real world. Well, *my* real world. This was her now, her normal-time, passing for her in the tank the same as here. There was only so long her body could handle the deprivation and stasis of the suspension fluid.

Much longer than I'd managed it, mind you. Pride filled me for being correct when I saw her potential as a child—for once, pride, not for myself. She had exceeded even my brilliance and my expectations for her.

Working independently, my mind had already deduced another crucial difference between my machine and hers: when she had to leave, no part of her would remain here. She hadn't created a new world as my machine evidently did. Here, Sabrina Hollister doesn't exist—nor does Jessica Matthews. They cannot stay behind, to stay with me, when Sabrina will have left.

Here will remain one lonely elderly man grieving yet another loss.

Fortunately for me, this time, the mourning wouldn't endure for long. You see, I was already at the end of the life expectancy on which my cardiologist and hepatologist agreed. My brilliant daughter had made her journey to see me just in time. 'In Time.' What an ironic way to describe anything, knowing how we, father and daughter scientists, working in different worlds and at diverse times, had shattered the illusions of what time had been understood to be since, well, the dawn of time.

"Daddy, I'm so happy to see you again—so ecstatic my adaptations to your invention worked. I haven't been able to test it as you did your machine, so I… I guess I took a leap of faith when I entered it."

"Wait. Is this your first time in the tank? And for this long? You have no idea what your mental or physical state will be when you wake up?"

"No. It wasn't possible to test. I skipped from prototype to human trial. And… here I am."

"Sweetheart, can you end it early? Can you send yourself back?"

"AI simulations based on the most credible theories say killing myself here won't work. In my tank, the mental anguish would likely kill me."

"You must have thought of it. What if I were dead when you arrived? What if you hadn't been able to meet me? You must have had a way out." In sending herself here without proper testing, she'd been reckless, but not having an escape plan, a way back until the time ran out—no, not my daughter. "I know because *I* would, *I did*, from an overlap. Tell me you can end this and get out of that tank before you suffer any damage in your world."

"I can. Well, I *had* a callback button."

"*No*—don't tell me. The key fob I destroyed."

"The mirror. The fob was to my rental car."

"Breanie, I'm so sorry. There must be another way. I'm terribly frightened for how long your body and mind have been in the crossover tank."

"Don't be. I have an insane number of monitors hooked to me, and a medical team watching over me. They can call me back in the event of a serious threat to my health. Besides, my time is almost up."

Bitter-sweet. I'd heard that before without fully understanding the expression. I thought it may have applied every time I entered the chamber, sweet for the opportunity to spend new time with my Ellie while bitter as I entered knowing it would end. In the reality of normal-time, we know all things must end. That irresistible optimism and relentless hope woven into the human spirit suppresses such notions.

Ellie and I were going to live forever.

I suppose most young, and not so young, couples in love must feel the same. Invincible because we refuse to face the inevitability of our destination—just as I had buried an irrefutable fact: my time with Sabrina now would end.

26 | The Plan

LATE night slipped undetected into early morning. Sabrina had dozed off, leaning into my side, my arm around her. A picture of a life I once led in an overlap I thought had ended twenty years ago. My daughter became a woman yet sat beside me as a twelve-year-old girl, full of life, dreams, and the wonder of expectation.

When that near-teen girl cuddled up beside me that last time, just before I had been yanked out of the greatest moments of my life—only not my life, a short-lived overlap of a pretend family I never had—I had no such dreams or expectations for her. In my selfishness, I'd created lives only to be tragically cut short by the limitations of my body in the suspension chamber.

Admittedly, I still struggled, against all evidence of Sabrina's existence, to wrap my head around an overlap continuing once I'd left it. I exhausted my sleepy brain on the physics and ended with nothing but the warmth of my Breanie beside me as proof. She was real. She was alive.

She was about to go.

The three o'clock herbal infusion she prepared stretched the conversation closer to dawn. She updated me on George's life since I left. He'd married and had a child, making me a grandfather. Of course, she had no photos to show me as her true self lay naked in a thick, gooey liquid in her real world. I basked in the pride for him radiating from her face as she told me of his accomplishments as an English professor and successful independent author of science-fiction novels.

"Funny, he's authored these amazing stories about impossible fantastic science and amazing futures with detailed world-building. He writes about aliens, time travel, and even one story about parallel worlds. I've never been into such stories, but, of course, I've read his. He's quite good at character arcs and dialogue." She took my hand and turned a saddened gaze to me. "He just couldn't accept that you were here and I could travel across to see you."

"Sweetheart, you've been in your tank for so long. Where do Mom and George think you are?"

"Mom knows I'm working on something and thinks its function helps me explore time. I told her I'd be away for a while experimenting in it."

"For months? She accepted that?"

"Not readily, no. It's why Mom doesn't know the location of my lab. I have my team sending her updates, so she knows I'm not dead."

"And George? Wouldn't he notice your… sabbatical?"

"I told him exactly what I was doing. I can only guess what he's thinking now. I think he'd accept me telling him I'd been abducted by aliens and experimented on before he believed this."

"I wish I could see him. See your mom again."

"I tried, Dad, believe me. I could have come here sooner but delayed, stubbornly trying to find a way to get you back into that overlap. Your technology simply doesn't allow it without a memory from this world. And if you could reenter a previous overlap, you'd live it differently from that point on."

"But your machine works on a different set of parameters."

"True. My adaptations are completely different. The evidence suggests, after detailed structured hypotheses and countless AI projection models, it only connected me here because of you."

"What do you mean?"

"The theory on which my machine is based cannot scan alternate dimensions, the other universes created by the overlaps. I can only see through to this reality in the chamber because of your DNA in me. See, I jumped into this world because of our connection."

"If anyone besides you or George tried it, they'd be unable to. Because they don't have an anchor point here."

"Exactly. I'm working on some exceptions that have yet to pan out. I'm afraid my findings have been conclusive on being unable to send anyone from here to my world. Not even you, who created it."

"When you napped, just before, I ran multiple advanced calculations combining my machine with what you told me of your modifications. A few times, I thought I had it—a way to send me back. Each one hit a wall at some point."

"And your health. Dad, I don't think you'd survive a trip, not even in your machine as it was before you destroyed them all."

"I'd certainly not pass the required pre-travel physical."

"Wait." Sabrina paused with blank eyes, as I did when I entered a trance of deep thought. "Why were you running those calculations? If none of your machines exist any longer…?" My smile gave me away. "You kept one, didn't you?"

"I have a lab below my bedroom. You didn't think that massive solar array we walked by yesterday was just to power this tiny home, did you?"

"You've still been using it? In your condition."

"I hadn't entered it in years. Truthfully, I've not used it much since your overlap, after my time with Ellie raising a family, falling in love with her again, *and* with you and George. Then, having to leave. I lost the desire to continue torturing myself. And to think about having children again, only to leave them. No, that last machine has had little use until recently."

"You used it recently? Dad, it could have killed you."

"Just a short trip to a memory of a weekend in Florence with your mom. Well, I guess not, as it was a new overlap, not *your* mom, exactly."

A hand came over mine, sandwiching it between both of hers. "Why would you risk it?"

"When I saw you, that video interview. I just had to go back to see Ellie again, close to your age. I had to be sure my memory hadn't betrayed me. You look so much alike but for such subtle differences."

"The nose and chin, I know. Mom always says how happy she is I didn't get those from her."

"You are both the most beautiful creatures I've ever seen. I really thought my plan had a chance at success. Just another failure."

"Your plan? You mean your groggy middle-of-the-night sofa calculations?"

"I've done some of my best work in the wee hours and with a scotch to wake the brain."

A shared laugh conquered the melancholy over not being able to do more, to travel back with Sabrina to see George and Ellie as they were now. My darling daughter had the same mind, only sharper, and not only compared to me in my old age. She asked me to recount all my mental calculations and sofa theorizing, giving each failed direction rapt attention.

With the technical dialogue concluded Sabrina again cuddled into me and wrapped me in her arms. We both took a nap for a few hours and woke to a bright, sunny morning. Over espresso, we returned to our catch-up talk about our lives since we were together so long ago, literally in another life for me.

"Daddy." Eyes full of longing pierced my soul. "One thing I'm not sure about… I know I'm in the tank. My body didn't physically travel here. Yet I woke in this world in physical form—naked in a park in the middle of the day, that was fun—and when I go back…?"

"You're unsure if you'll disappear like a Jedi or leave your lifeless body behind."

"Exactly." She chuckled. "I hadn't thought of Jedi since the last time you made me watch that old film. But yeah. I don't want to leave you having to deal with that."

"I think I'd rather not as well. But if that's the price for this magical couple of days, I'll deal with it."

"I think you'll know soon. I feel that tingle, you know. Your machine did it, too. When you entered, it latched onto the memory's temporal orientation, then again just before it ended."

"We have so much more to say. I… I don't want this to end."

"I'm sorry, Daddy." Tear-filled eyes looked soulfully into mine. "I didn't want to hurt you by showing up unannounced and leaving like this. I'd hoped to find you sooner and have more time."

"Can't you come back?" I knew the answer, yet I had to ask.

"No. Like your machine, mine cannot repeat a trip. I have no overlaps to create, just one jump to your world and one jump back. It's more a limitation of my body than the machine. I'm sorry."

"Don't be. You've given me such a gift. I couldn't have imagined it. I love you, Baby Girl."

"I love you so much, Daddy. I'm so glad I got to see you again."

My Sabrina's skin began to glow, and my sleepy eyes took a moment to realize it wasn't the morning's sunlight on her flesh. Her trip had reached its end. We embraced.

"I love you, Breanie. I love you so much."

I clutched an empty dress against my chest.

27 | The Failure

WHEN I studied those pale blue, almost gray eyes—so wide and round as they took in the world's light for the first time—I knew. Sabrina's mind would outperform my own, far exceeding my accomplishments. In her childhood, she'd shown such obvious signs of brilliance, her genius shining through in her earliest ideas for new inventions and improved methods of doing everyday tasks.

I'd learned of her life after I left. She funded her research not on my fortune left behind but on her own successful creation of a new augmented reality experience that overtook *trænSɛnd*, reducing it to the 'poor man's version' of her system. She called it *The Overlap*, a fully immersive four-dimensional AR experience. It took her less than two years to develop and sell the patent, making her a millionaire before her eighteenth birthday.

As an adult, her brain mystified me. When I shared my wee-hours musings over her improved machine and how I tried to bend quantum physics yet again to my will, she offered her observations and theories. I had no doubt she could figure it out, find a way to get me back into her world, not as an overlap, not starting over, but rejoining them as they were.

We didn't have that time to work together.

I could have blamed the age, my deteriorated cerebral capacity, the dull edge that my former mental sharpness had developed like a knife with years of use without sharpening or honing—the solution rested outside my reach. Not even a younger me would have cracked it. I doubted Sabrina would either. What did people say with their expressions? 'Two heads are better than one.'

Honestly, I never bought into that. Before Sabrina, I'd never found a head equal to my own, or that added anything productive to my work or creative process. Peter? He only got in the way. Some called him the 'Steve Jobs' to my 'Wozniak.' I resented that. Not only was Peter never near as brilliant as Jobs, but also because what I accomplished could never be compared to making simple computer systems.

Revolutionaries? Sure, we had that in common. I cannot deny what other creatives and industry pioneers have done before me. That Apple continued to thrive and would outlast me… *Come to think of it; people will be using Apple products long after my machine has been forgotten.*

Where was I?

Failure.

I should have been used to that by now. While some of my biggest failures had spawned my greatest successes, many got tossed in the trash, rubbish to be discarded. Without Sabrina's mind working with me, I'd see nothing but failure in trying to augment my last working machine to send me home to reunite me with my family. Fifteen more years dangled like a carrot before me, but like an aged horse that needed to be put down, I'd never feel its satisfying crunch between my teeth.

Granted, my stubbornness retained all the strength of its youth, so I didn't stop trying. Days with limited sleep and too much coffee ended with the same brick wall. I hit it every time. Maybe two great minds, hers greater than mine, could break through it or take down the wall brick by brick.

Not alone.

Yes, I had been kidding myself. No way existed in the most twisted and stretched definitions of nature, physics, quantum mechanics, or fringe science that would accomplish the impossible. Some things sat just beyond reach in the realm of disbelief I had fought my entire life: accepting something as not doable.

Failure.

Yet again, I had failed. I supposed that might have humbled a 'normal' person. I knew I had walked a different path that took me far from normal all my life. Perhaps that made me so unlikable to most 'normal' people. You see, my isolation hadn't been solely my choice. Those who knew me best had fully agreed with my conclusion that I needed no friends and they did not need me.

Ellie saw me.

I suppose that was why I couldn't let her go. No one else saw the good man in me she loved. I never considered myself a good man, but my love's relentless affection nearly convinced me I had a soul.

Sabrina brought that same humanity back to me. Even Jessica had awoken that cooled ember into a spark. When I found in Jessica my Breanie's heart, the same fire burned deep inside me beyond any I had felt in even the best of my overlaps with Ellie.

Save one, the one with Sabrina and George.

Desperation kept me working on the calculations long after the conclusion became obvious. For the first time in decades, it brought me to the basement not to use my machine but to break it down to pieces and try to re-work it based on theories my brilliant daughter had rightly debunked.

It would have been devastating to see my machine reduced to useless parts scattered over the lab floor under any previous circumstance. As I had already resolved not to use it again, not to risk creating a new world, my misery came from a new ache deep in my heart. I finally admitted defeat. I'd not see my Sabrina again. Not see the man George had become or meet my grandson. Never again would I hold my precious Ellie in my arms.

While I knew it and welcomed it weeks before, now, the thought of dying alone brought a frightening chill over me. In all those worlds I created, how many times had I, would I, die alone?

Perhaps that's where I found my greatest failure. And in it, I found one last success of sorts.

"Majel… Access backdoor protocol to military installations. Run remote shutdown and self-destruct protocols on all remaining units."

28 | The Empty House

MY HOME had been a refuge from the world, from my life. From myself. Just me and my memories, as I thought I wanted it. Of course, Guillaume and Samantha came in and out, no more genuine company than Majel. Then Jessica Matthews entered the house and rekindled embers I'd thought dwindled out of existence long ago, and loneliness became an unwelcome companion.

Sense of it came in the mind-shattering manifestation of the still unbelievable truth of her identity as my little Breanie. With Sabrina gone, the home reverted to a house, a structure of isolation, the prison where I'd soon die.

Alone.

Two weeks had passed when a medical team came for a checkup despite my adamant and persistent refusal to have the visit. Majel let them in. You see, a stubbornness in my AIA came from my personality and thought patterns being scanned into it during its programming. It sometimes disobeyed when doing so protected its master. That second law of robotics is at war with my override protocols in the digital mind I created. I could have ignored the legal requirements dictating incorporation of Asimov's so-called safety protocols, but having my assistant protect my life was a choice I didn't wish to side-step when I wrote its code.

'La donna è mobile.' I suppose that's why I chose the female voice for my assistant and sole conversational partner for far too many years.

'Something for the pain,' they told me—nothing for the finality of my situation. I always loathed variables and indefinity. I preferred to deal with hard facts and definitive conclusions. So, as you can imagine, when they told me I had anywhere from a couple of days to three weeks, I politely threw them out of my house.

The emptiness I thought I'd enjoyed now stiffened me in an irritable discomfort like fingernails relentlessly scratching down a chalkboard. Maddeningly constant.

I explained to Guillaume and Samantha that they weren't being fired. I wished to die alone as I had lived. I saw no need for these strangers I'd known for three decades to be there to deal with my decaying corpse. I'd arranged everything in advance with a funeral home, and Majel had been instructed to let them in and what digital documents to provide.

I also left Guillaume, and Samantha set for life with ridiculously generous severance packages. They'd not have to work another day in their lives. Heck, their grandchildren wouldn't ever have to work. However, I encouraged them to ensure their progeny developed healthy self-respect from arduous work and earning what they had, as they each had done.

What about my secretly kept machine in the hidden sublevel of my house? Majel was equipped with a self-destruct that would leave barely a trace of the home and its items, including that infernal machine—my greatest failure. Of course, I had to give her an upload location so it wouldn't pull that third-law rubbish on me and fail the self-destruct to preserve its own existence. Majel will long outlive me running the systems on the next model of the International Space Station.

And all the money, what's left of it? My final act of philanthropy. My last will and testament directed every cent to be donated to the Ellie Hollister Foundation. It cared for children in need and assisted victims of crimes and various other unfortunate events for almost half a century. Some comfort for my wasted life doing some good and for Ellie's heart of gold to go on helping people. Her legacy would outlive and outshine mine.

Drizzle fell over a silvery-gray morning.

Sitting in my Chesterfield, I twirled the tumbler in my hand and let my fingertips examine the textured pattern in the crystal they knew so well. Other than the smokey aroma, I didn't partake. Since Sabrina's visit, my thirst for it had abated. I still poured two a day and sometimes sipped it.

"Majel… I want to dictate something. It'll be long and may need some editing to polish up."

"Ready for dictation."

"Pause."

I collected my thoughts and double-checked them to verify I wanted to do what I was about to do. I did. I meant it when I said my story needed to be told. I wished Jessica Matthews to tell it, but that didn't pan out as the reporter turned out to be a clever alter ego of my Sabrina.

Majel would have to do. She'd tell my story.

"Majel. Recall the recording from the visit of Jessica Matthews. As I dictate, fill in the gaps with details from those transcripts. I wish you to write my memoir from my words and those logs. Credit the author as Jessica Matthews and publish it. All proceeds are to go to Ellie's foundation."

"Acknowledged. Ready for dictation."

The better part of two and a half days had Majel transcribing my ramblings, editing, adding details and dialogue from the logs of Jessica's visit—my time with Sabrina—and reading it back to me.

"Majel. Save the memoir and hold. Add relevant events from my last moments and record my passing. Wait one year from then to publish the book and make it available worldwide in every publishable language."

"Acknowledged."

That night, I slept in my chair, lacking the energy or desire to move to the bedroom. My custom Chesterfield offered some reclining, and I found it more comfortable than being flat on the bed in my currently frail state of health. After a coffee and a few biscuits, I returned to my favorite view, faithfully entering the room through the large glass pane beside the chair in my study.

The sunrise had lied about it being a cloudless day, and the light rain had intensified somewhat. I closed my eyes to gentle drumbeats of droplets pelting the glass.

"Excuse me, Marcus." Majel always spoke graciously and on a first-name basis. "You have a visitor."

"Majel. What have I told you? You know my strict no-visitor rule."

"May I quote the second law of robotics and artificial intelligence?"

"*Azimov*," I grumbled.

"Unclear. Please repeat your request."

"If it's the doctors, that law doesn't apply, they can't save me. Send them away."

"Your visitor is identified as Jessica Matthews."

29 | The Visitor

HOW could she have done it? After months in the tank at risk to her health and her life, and with no known way to return here when she left, how could she be back? It had been just over two weeks. No, the physical limitations of human flesh and the brain's ability to sustain a reality while the body remained in stasis simply wouldn't allow it. Yet she was here.

Bringing me to dizzying euphoria, Sabrina came back.

Soon enough, I felt Spector's approach like a warm breath on my neck. I'd been fully convinced the next time I closed my eyes would be the last.

Now, they must never close, I resolved.

I had the duration of her tube ride from the road to make myself presentable. One of the advantages of isolation was not having anyone to present yourself to, allowing certain hygienic liberties. Yes, I know. I took the long way around to prevent saying I had become lazy. I tried to remember the last time I brushed my teeth. Surely, it couldn't have been days.

Lifting myself from the chair had increased in difficulty daily. The effort alone would have been beyond the reach of my worn-out bones and tired muscles. Years ago, I saw this coming and had the lifting mechanism built into the Chesterfield.

The ruffle of dragging slippers too heavy to be raised off the smooth tile played like the introduction to a symphony in my ears. It was a pleasant announcement of the joyous experience about to unfold, and I needed to dress up for the occasion.

My Breanie. One last opportunity to look upon her face.

To hold her.

Freshly pressed pants hid the sagging pale skin that had lost its grip on the flesh beneath. My white button-down shirt hung loose over my torso. The only benefit I saw from my illnesses was finally reducing the beer belly effect of the scotch and sloth-like lifestyle I'd lived for far too long.

I hadn't shaved and never cared for the stubble look. Once, I tried to grow a beard in an overlap, and it hung from my face like a stringy mess of frayed wire bunched into lumps. Now, it appeared like old cobwebs stretched over a basement wall. I made the skin beneath, almost a grayish hue, smooth and hairless by my blade, and washed the remnants of shaving cream from my face.

A most unusual noise, pleasant and close to forgotten, danced across my ears. I then realized I started humming. It was a tune from one of Melody Buonavoce's classics. Such a jovial surge of energy hadn't invigorated my spirits since Sabrina's departure. Expectation for her return banished the terminal illness and stripped me of all its pains.

Of course, I knew this would be the encore, the final curtain about to close on my unusual life. All the lives I'd led would soon be forgotten.

"Majel. Be sure to keep recording and add these final moments to my memoirs."

"Acknowledged."

I wondered if anyone would care. Once *Vacations in Time* closed its doors for good, why did anyone have to even think of Marcus Hollister? And when they learn about the life I lived, the horrible things my machine allowed, and worse, as I recently learned from Sabrina, the overlaps of tens of thousands of peoples' trips in the chamber… What would anyone think of me?

My legacy.

What did it matter?

Soon, I'd be gone, and the legacy of Ellie would endure. Her foundation will continue to impact so many lives positively, helping millions across the globe. That's my legacy, even if kept secret, to let the light of my dearest love shine unextinguished for all time.

"Majel. Be sure to omit any reference to me in connection with Ellie's foundation. Nothing about the funding. Just mention in the book's dedication how proud I am of her and how she goes on helping people well beyond her tragic ending."

"Acknowledged."

I took the remaining minutes the tube capsule demanded to reach the house to add recent musings to Majel's record of my memoir dictation. With teeth brushed and hair combed—it had easily been many days since I'd cared enough to neaten my hair—I returned to my loyal companion of thirty years, my chair, to await my joy, my darling's farewell visit.

Closure.

Perhaps for her as much as me.

The so-called experts merge physical, emotional, and mental health studies into advice that should be taken with a spoonful of salt. All agreed we needed it. I never could get closure in my life. I supposed just the opposite. My life in normal-time ended with Ellie under that streetlight. Each overlap I entered had to end abruptly, unfulfilled. Each time, a new loss, pain, and chapter opened without a proper ending.

Now Sabrina would give me that—closure.

She got something from our time together as well. I only wish the reality of who I had become could have been less disappointing for her. Did she come here expecting to find an accomplished man of science living the highlife? Did the reality fail her imagination of finding a man she could be proud to call Dad? A good man?

Had I been a good man?

Perhaps my mental rambling was the 'normal' part of dying everyone experienced when they saw its outstretched arm nearing, closing the gap between life and death. I don't suppose my Ellie had time for such, as sudden as her demise had fallen upon her–upon us.

Anxious minutes arrested me in suspense. *That darn capsule's too slow.*

Oh.

"Majel. Make *absolutely* sure Jessica Matthews is out of the house before you begin the self-destruct."

"May I quote the first law of robotics and artificial intelligence?"

"Majel. Shut up."

"Would you like me to carry out that order before or after I inform you that your guest has arrived?"

How many times I've regretted adding that snarky bite to her personality.

"Let her in."

"I did."

Eager eyes left the window's panorama to see the silhouette in the archway from the dining room. I hadn't bothered to turn on any lights, having opted to invite the gloom of the day to sit with me in the study.

She brushed a curl behind her ear and paused.

I raised my chair to help me up and stood, arms open as an invitation.

She hesitated, then approached, considering each step. I observed the shadow and blueish-gray light work the lines of her face like Michelangelo's hammer and chisel, shaping and sculpting the work of art that was my daughter.

The nose. The chin.

"Ellie?"

30 | The Closure

HAD I had a heart of flame and lungs as elastic as balloons, I'd have floated like a zeppelin. Decades of longing, regret, and failure washed over me in fractions of a second. Maybe it was death. All those zealots and hopefuls out there, desperate for something more, something after. Could they have been right all along?

Reunited soulmates in an afterlife of bliss?

No. Normal-time. I was in normal-time, and my Ellie stood before me. A version of her unlike any these eyes had ever seen. Lovely as ever, as every Ellie had always been. I lost myself in the symmetry of her face, gentle lines carved where her skin had always been taut.

"Hello, Marcus, my love."

"Ellie? Is it you … Is it really you?"

"In the flesh. Somehow. That daughter of yours got all your brains and then some."

"She did indeed - She did indeed."

"After all this time… aren't you going to hold me?"

With an extended inhale, I pulled her into myself. The familiarity of the sensation, the rightness of it, filled me with strength long since retired from my body. I hadn't been on my feet this long in about a week.

Her scent, her hair, awakened as in a memory or overlap, entered me like a drug. For the first time since that attack, now with over half a century gone by, my Ellie existed with me in normal-time. The tear-filled embrace endured for hours but likely ended in minutes. I never wanted her hands to come away from my back, rubbing over my shoulder blades as she always did before clamping onto my shoulders and squeezing.

"Let me look on you." That cadence. The voice of an angel, my angel, fell upon my ears. "You got old."

Chuckles escaped our mouths and eased the charged emotion to a level that hopefully wouldn't overwhelm my weak heart and kill me.

"It's been fifty years."

"Just over twenty for me, my love, when you left me. *This* me."

"Every *you* has been you. The years have been gentler on you."

"I haven't had as many as you've had."

"Of course, you must be in your sixties now. A grandma."

"And you're a grandpa. I ache to think how much you've missed with us."

"Let's sit… on the sofa. I'm…"

"I know. Sabrina told me." We sat almost on top of each other, maintaining an embrace. "It's why I made her prep me and the machine so quickly. I couldn't believe it when she told me, but the fire in her, the love for her father, for you, radiated from her as I hadn't seen since you left."

"You mean since the me left behind died."

"No. Sabrina had a wonderful relationship with that *you*. They loved each other dearly and continued to work together. Inseparable, as you were with her. Yet I saw something in her change. I couldn't know it at the time, having had no idea about your machine, you coming from here, creating the overlap you called it. I thought it the normal changes as she became a teenager."

"She knew a part of her dad had gone. I thought you all had gone. Oh, Ellie, my love, please believe me… I had no idea what my trips in the machine were doing, leaving versions of everyone behind."

"She told me that, too. And I agree with her. My sweet Marcus, we are so grateful for the life you gave us and the time we spent with you. And for the lives we continue to have, to be alive. Never feel bad about giving us that."

"She did what I never could—increased her time in the tank. It's why I never got more than about fifteen years. Why I had to leave you, leave Sabrina and George."

"I know. As you can imagine, we had intense discussions as we prepped for my trip."

"How long have you been here? It took her months to find me and get an appointment. Of course, I had no idea who she was."

"I arrived yesterday. Just as naked in the same park. She thought it would go that way—something about quantum relativity putting me in the same place. You know I never got or cared for that scientific stuff."

"I thought you were her. My AIA said Jessica Matthews was here. That was her alter ego in this world."

"She told me to use it. She hoped the likeness would get me by your assistant. I thought it told you. When it opened the gate and directed me into the capsule… it called me *Ellie*."

"She's a clever one, that Majel. She figured it out and let you in before I cleared Jessica Matthews through. *Oh.* Sabrina… said only she or George could possibly make the trip to this universe. Because they carry my DNA, linking them physically to this reality, to me. How'd you get…"

My untimely cough caught Ellie unawares. She got me some water.

"I insisted it would work. Sabrina balked at the idea— what did I know about all this, right? Perhaps she did some tests to humor me and agreed that no harm would come to me in her machine if it failed. I'd just wake up."

"Well, I must consider the science, you know that. My brain won't let it pass. I followed the DNA link explanation. You and I, as 'one' as we are, we share no DNA."

"My dearest love… we share something much stronger."

While my logical brain had much more to refute on that point, I locked it in a box to give myself fully to this unexpected marvel. My Ellie, the mother of my children and the love of my life, sat here with me. We talked for hours about shared memories and experiences separated by years and universes.

While I clearly perceived her love and affection for Daniel in her mention of him, her second husband, Ellie's eyes didn't shine as much as when she retold memories we had in common. Immense gratitude for him being there for her when I and the leftover me—no, that's a poor way to think of it—left her alone filled me with joy. She had been happy, she was happy, even in her second widowhood. She lived a rich and rewarding life as a mother and grandmother and devoted her brilliant legal mind to helping those unjustly imprisoned to gain freedom.

I swelled with pride and satisfaction.

On how many worlds had this magnificent person left such a legacy? I resigned myself to accepting I'd not be able to say I had been a good man in any of my lives. Knowing I'd had a hand in creating worlds where my amazing Ellie was leaving her mark was legacy enough for me.

My sweetheart and true love prepared meals and cared for me through the day and that night. We hardly slept, though my spirit lost the battle to the flesh several times, and I dozed off. Each time, waking in lost love's warm embrace.

"Ellie. I can't… just can't believe this is real, that you're here. Thank you so much for this. I only regret you finding me as I am. An old man in need of care."

"I had to come. You've no idea what this means to me."

"I think I do. You and I are the only two people alive on countless worlds who could know how we feel now."

"True. Would you like me to make some breakfast?"

"No." I took Ellie's hand and laid a second over it as Sabrina had done to me two weeks prior. I looked longingly into her eyes, those pools of sorrow and gratitude into which I fell. "I think it's best if you go. Did Sabrina give you a callback, a way to get home before the timer?"

"She told me how to get one, yes. Of course, I could take nothing here. Naked in a park, remember?" We shared a brief chortle. "She developed a failsafe I could make here with a simple mirror. But love, I'm not leaving you. We have time, time I wish not to end."

"I feel its approach, my love. I'll go quickly now." Even as I spoke, the grayness in the room thickened around me. I coughed again and had to spit into a tissue. "You shouldn't be here for this."

"I want to."

"You've given me everything, my dear, sweet Ellie. This, this has fulfilled me. This has allowed me to go in peace without regret. You gave me that, and I'm grateful. Now go, so your last memory of me isn't my final breath. Please, go."

I burst into a mess of tears I tried to hide. Equal forces tugged at my emotional core, one desperate for Ellie to stay by my side as long as possible, the other to spare her the sight.

"I've lost two husbands. Marcus, I wasn't there when you died. No one was. You went to face those… *mobsters*… alone. To save us, to save my life. I was at Daniel's side when he passed. So, you see, I have both experiences to draw on, and know I am staying here by your side."

"I've had both as well. I leaned over you as your life trickled away down the sewer drain in the gutter in a reddened current of fallen rain. And I lost you once, in an overlap. Sudden and out of my view."

"And which would you choose if you had to make that choice?"

How could I argue with Ellie? The scientific and mathematical genius of my mind had never been a match for her irrefutable logic. And she was correct. As gut-retching as it had been to be there with my normal-time Ellie, I was there with her, for her, reassuring her until the end. I'd not spare myself that agony to leave her abandoned, frightened, facing the unknown void alone.

Ellie wouldn't do that to me either.

Conversation about our children's lives and our grandson filled the last minutes we shared.

"Give all my love to George and little Marcus. And thank my Breanie again for me, for this. For her visit. For everything. Make sure she knows how proud I am of her."

"She does, my love. She knows."

Soft lips gently touched mine, and as the world faded from my dulled eyes, a calm swept through me, assuring me it was enough to be a hero to the people who really mattered.

THANK YOU

As an indie writer, people finding my stories and reading them is the greatest reward. I hope you enjoyed this touching story of regret and loss. While some of Marcus' experiences and feelings may resonate with many of us, I believe there is hope for redemption, for that sought-after closure.

Some of this story comes from my losses, desperate desires, and hopes for a reunion. What I love about writing is taking elements of myself to create deep characters with impactful stories.

If you enjoyed this novella, please consider taking a few minutes to leave a review. Reviews are critical for an indie author to be found and allow other readers to enjoy their stories.

I greatly appreciate your support as a reader.

Thank you for your review.

Please consider following my writing and getting news, advanced synopses, preview chapters of upcoming works, and connecting with me at www.glassauthor.com.

OTHER BOOKS BY THE AUTHOR

The New Europa trilogy is a story of life's challenges in a small Mars colony after two centuries. Conspiracy theories spread, and the seeds of social unrest are actively fertilized and watered by disgruntled individuals and small groups determined to 'get the truth out there.'

In *Colony's Dawn,* our protagonist, Gift Ojo, struggles to overcome her initial dismissal of any issues, desperately clinging to her belief that life is fine and everyone works for the colony's good. When suspicions cement and acts of sabotage ensue, she must become something more, an unwitting hero to rally her friends and save her colony.

All Lies is a New Europa novella best read after *Colony's Dawn*. It tells the origin of the group Raffaela discovered and the role they came to play in the overarching conspiracy that rocked the foundations of Gift's happy colony. Your gift for joining my newsletter at www.glassauthor.com

In *Colony's Fall,* our characters' world expands into something they never could have imagined. Along with the marvels and wonder come new and horrific tests of their humanity, threatening their existence.

In *Colony's End,* we follow Gift on her journey to grow into her own person to face all-out war. Will she have what it takes to stand against her people and find her choice, a solution to stop the endless cycle of humanity fighting and killing each other?

ABOUT THE AUTHOR

N Joseph Glass

An Italian American born in New York and living in Milan, Italy. As a sci-fi fan, I enjoy interesting stories that fire the imagination. I love the genres of science fiction, action/adventure, and thrillers. I lose myself reading compelling novels and have taken inspiration to create characters and expound my stories from being captivated by reading series such as Foundation, Dune, and The Expanse.

My journey to creative writing has just happened. As ideas entered my mind, I began visualizing scenes and the people in them. As my imagination added detail and depth, I put my fingers on my keyboard and started writing. Creativity became a cherished hobby at first.

Optimistic views of the future through art always interest me, as I believe ours will be bright.

www.glassauthor.com